A

PERFECT

EYE

STEPHANIE KANE

COLD HARD PRESS
Denver, Colorado

Seeds of Doubt
Colorado Authors League Award Winner

"Kane deserves to join the ranks of the big-time legal-thriller eagles."
– Publishers Weekly

"Kane's background as a defense attorney informs the legal thriller backbone of the story, but the exploration of childhood sins, whether monstrous or incidental, gives *Seeds of Doubt* its emotional heft."
– The Baltimore Sun

"Deftly written."
– Chicago Sun

"One of the outstanding mysteries of the year."
– The Cleveland Plain-Dealer

Extreme Indifference
Colorado Book Award Winner
Colorado Authors League Award Winner

"Sturdy intrigue in and out of court with an especially sharp eye for the riptides of power running just beneath the legal quiddities."
– Kirkus Reviews

"Fast-moving and intriguing. Kane knows both her protagonist and the legal terrain well."
– San Francisco Chronicle

"A tight, well-written thriller with an ending that caught me completely off-balance."
– The Cleveland Plain-Dealer

Quiet Time

"Stephanie Kane does it again. *Quiet Time* keeps your mind thinking and your heart racing – What a great read!"
– Rikki Klieman, Court TV

"Life's greatest dramas play out in family life. The end is riveting and a surprise—but that's what Kane is all about."
– The Denver Post

"Stephanie Kane is a terrific storyteller who knows how to grab the attention of the audience and keeps it."
– The Midwest Book Review

A PERFECT EYE

First Edition
First Printing, 2019

Cold Hard Press
Denver, CO

Book interior design by Susan Brooks
Cover design by Marcel Venter

Library of Congress Number: 2019901391

ISBN Print: 978-1-7336715-0-7
ISBN: Digital: 978-1-7336715-1-4

Printed in the United States of America

For John

It began on a Saturday morning walk when she was five, right after her mom died. Like musical chairs, he suddenly stopped. *Tell me what you see, Lily.* A house with a fence. *What else?* A truck. *What color?* Red. They walked another two blocks. *What did you see before?* They retraced their steps. *What do you see now?* Paw prints in the grass, and a place where the dog had sat waiting for its master. Each time she saw more: a shiny tab from a soda can in the gutter; traces of pink on the sidewalk from hopscotch, scoured by rain. Next week he tested her again. *What's different from before?* The dog has a chew-bone. *What else?* A new hopscotch game! *Details, please...* When she was ten, he took her to a museum.

Your eye's like perfect pitch, he said. *You're lucky you were born with it.*

Chapter One

Lily looped her apple-green lanyard around her neck and pushed through the revolving door at the entrance to the Denver Art Museum. On this May morning, the Kurtz Building's titanium panels gleamed and its steel prow evoked a spaceship on a pit stop in the middle of downtown. *Welcome to Starship Galactica.*

"Sorry I couldn't grab coffee for us," she told the guard inside the door. The stuff across the plaza was better than the cafeteria's.

He winked. "No problem, Ms. Sparks."

The Conservator of Paintings could not be late for the docent training tour—not when the subject was a masterpiece by Impressionist artist Gustave Caillebotte.

She crossed to the main building and stopped at the European & American gallery's threshold. The thrill of gazing at *Fields of the Gennevilliers Plain, No. Seven* never got old. The last in Caillebotte's acclaimed series of landscapes painted near his retreat north of Paris, it had been lost for more than a century. Now its wind-swept grasses and wildflowers, its massing clouds, and the man in the brimmed hat hurrying home from the field drew countless visitors and graced the museum's T-shirts, mousepads and coffee cups. But to her, *Seven* was more than an attraction that sold merchandise.

Gris-clair, the light cloud canopy under which Caillebotte painted, intensified the painting's tone. His vermillion and chrome yellow had caught more than the pastoral beauty of poppies and grass; their very radiance hinted at hubris. In a canvas less than two feet square, he'd captured the drama of poplars standing watch in midground and the man's urgency to reach the red roofs in the distance. Would he beat the storm? *Seven* reminded her that nature was fickle and Eden an illusion. That in the blink of an eye, what she thought she knew could vanish and all she held dear could be lost.

A dozen docent trainees—"provisionals" in museum-speak—were being addressed by Dr. Gina Wheelock, Curator of Paintings, in her stilettos and a slinky black sheath. Curators and conservators were the museum's top non-administrative dogs, and she and Gina technically occupied the same status. But to Gina a painting was less important than psychoanalyzing the artist, and now she was laying it on as thick as Caillebotte's impasto.

"...so fortunate that The Kurtz Foundation donated this iconic treasure. Here we sense none of the alienation of Caillebotte's blue-grey cityscapes, the tortured perspectives of his iron bridges and rainy Paris streets—"

"The guys with umbrellas and top hats?" said a voice from the back.

Gina blinked rapidly. The interruption came from Nick, the only male provisional who was under sixty—and cute. She quickly regained her train of thought. "Yes, those paintings were earlier. Throughout his career Caillebotte was misunderstood. Now back to *Seven*..."

Lily's assistant Amy, whose copper tresses were braided in a crown and cascaded down like a girl in a pre-Raphaelite portrait, stood with senior docent Dave, a retired chemist as barrel-chested as a Dutch burgher. Dave whispered something and Amy stifled a giggle. Armed with their own green lanyards and printed Talking with Visitors Points, some of the provisionals were already looking at their watches and yawning while Gina droned on.

"...so-called lost years in Petit-Gennevilliers ..."

Gina's hair was short and spiky, with edgy dark roots and platinum strands frosted and moussed like snakes—*psychoanalyze that*. She stood less than a foot from the painting, her blue-red nails digging into her bony forearms. Lily had to talk to her about that; *Seven* deserved better than to be breathed or coughed on. Gina leaned forward, her face now inches from the canvas.

"...scudding clouds and fertile fields. Don't you wish you could enter Caillebotte's paradise and inhale its scents?"

Gina sneezed.

Shit.

Lily stepped forward and stopped at a respectful eighteen inches from *Seven*.

"I see Ms. Sparks decided to join us." Gina looked pointedly at her white-gold watch, then from Lily's Converse sneakers to her distressed jeans and ballcap cocked just so.

As for being late—not that it was any of Gina's business—that morning she'd taken her cat to the vet and had the puncture wounds to prove it. But the provisionals and *Seven* were what mattered. She smoothly picked up from her fuming colleague.

"Dr. Wheelock is quite right that *Seven* is Edenic. What makes it so is Caillebotte's touch." Dave shot her a thumb's up, and Amy shook her head. *That's not in the Talking Points.* Visitors were filtering in. Attracted by the crowd, some headed for *Seven*. "How did he create those cloud formations?"

"Color?" a retired librarian said.

"What else?" She waited. "Imagine Caillebotte standing next to you, painting those clouds. You think he was satisfied with them?"

The yawning had stopped. The trainees weren't just listening; they were looking. The librarian peered closer at the painting. Her face broke into a delighted smile. "The impasto's thicker there."

"Yes! Instead of scraping off the pigment, Caillebotte kept adding more layers." The trainees moved closer, but not *too* close. Lily looked from face to face. Now they were starting to see. She pointed to the vertical line bisecting the field. "How did he create this furrow?"

"He scored it with his palette knife," Nick said.

"Good. What does the depth of that scoring tell you?"

"Caillebotte was angry?" the librarian offered.

"Maybe." Gina was giving her that stony glare; this definitely wasn't in the Talking Points. But the trainees had to forge their own relationships with *Seven,* to feel it.

"He was frustrated with his inability to capture the scene?" Nick said.

"Exactly! Now for some fun…." An intern scurried up to Amy and whispered in her ear. Was something going on in the lab? Amy waved to get her attention, but she ignored her. "As for the scent of those fields, don't inhale too deeply. One of the marvels of modern Paris was its sewage system. It pumped its waste downstream. Caillebotte's Eden was actually a field of s—"

"Swamp gas?" Nick said with a sly wink.

He really was cute. Amy was making her way through the pack with a determined look on her face.

"Who's the guy with the hat?" someone asked.

Caillebotte's scurrying man.

"A thresher?" the librarian guessed.

Nick shook his head. "No scythe or sack."

The librarian squinted. "What kind of hat is that anyway?"

Amy clasped Lily firmly by the elbow. "So sorry for this tiny interruption," she announced, "but Ms. Sparks will rejoin you momentarily." Led by a seething Gina and still debating the hat, the trainees moved to a Monet and the visitors dispersed.

Lily followed Amy to the elevator. "What's so important?"

Amy pushed the button to go up. "An FBI agent's looking for you."

Her temples started to pound. The elevator pinged. Instead of getting on, she let the door close. "What does he want?"

"He didn't say." Amy's eyes narrowed. "But he knows you, and the intern said he's awfully good-looking."

Oh God, not him.

"What's his name?"

The elevator pinged again. Amy held the door, forcing her to get in.

"Paul Riley."

Chapter Two

The conservation lab was unnaturally quiet. A faint familiar scent—spicy, cloves?—wafted over solvents and varnish. As Lily walked past the Objects Conservator and her assistant, and the cubicles filled with interns and staff, necks craned. Paul had that effect on women.

Clean-shaven, short black hair in "Fed" style to match his impeccably tailored suit with its snowy pocket square and an athletic physique showing no trace of fat, he stood waiting in her office with his back to her. He reached up and slowly rubbed the back of his neck. Did he ever do that before?

"What do you want?" she said.

He turned with a start. Before his mask slipped back in place, she saw something different in his eyes. "Is that any way to greet an old colleague?"

Amy was listening in the doorway. Dave had followed her in and was getting an earful too. She had to cut this short.

"It's been a long time, Paul." *Ten years, three months and how many days?*

The clove was stronger now, his natural scent. The Armani tie wasn't one she'd given him, but the lushness of the silk reminded her that he'd given her something far more precious: her introduction to paintings, and through his eyes the gift of seeing them. Now he was looking at her intently.

"You cut it," he said.

"What?"

"Your hair."

Their last time together flashed through her head. In

bed at her condo, her cheek against the heat of his chest, caressing those tight curls just starting to gray, him running his fingers through her hair. His cell phone vibrating, him staring at the number before going into the bathroom to pick up.... She looked at his left hand now. Still no ring.

"You didn't answer my question," she said. "Why are you here?"

"I never thought you'd do it."

"Cut my hair?"

His gesture encompassed her office, with its cramped walls of treatises and binders and a wheeled ladder to reach the top shelf, to the floor-to-ceiling foot-wide window offering a sliver of view to the west. It stopped at her desk, with its lamp, tissue box, computer, pad and pens neatly aligned. "Everything in its place, just like when you were a lawyer."

"Thanks. There's a painting I'm about to clean—"

He glanced at Amy and Dave. "Can we speak privately?"

"No."

He rubbed his neck again. Tired, or did he need to do something with his hands?

"Okay," he said. "George Kurtz is dead."

Amy gasped.

"You're kidding!" Dave said.

"He was murdered last night at home."

"*What?*" Lily said.

She'd met the museum's benefactor and chairman of the board just once, at the gala two years earlier when *Seven* was unveiled. Their encounter was brief. Despite his age, Kurtz's attention was flattering. *You like champagne?* he asked. Without waiting for an answer, he signaled the waiter for another glass. There was something predatory about him. His avian stare—so at odds with his dignified demeanor and tuxedo—said he was attracted. He took her hand. His fingers were cold and clammy, his buffed nails sharp. His stare turned insulting. *Or perhaps something more?* When she still didn't respond, he'd looked past her for a more interesting conquest. Kurtz's death would throw the museum and the art world into turmoil, but why was Paul—

Dave jumped in again. "Did they steal his paintings?"

Paul didn't answer. But that explained his presence—sort of. He'd started as a federal prosecutor in D.C., then joined the FBI as one of the first agents assigned to its elite Art Theft Team. Stints at Homeland Security and the Counterterrorism and Forensic Science Research Unit followed; he was climbing the ladder fast. She'd seen an article about him consulting on the looting of artifacts from Syria and Iraq. But the FBI had other art experts.

"And Denver's such a hick town they had to call in the Feds," she said.

"Something like that."

"And you thought, give old Lily a call."

His smile was almost as insulting as Kurtz's. "There's a press conference this afternoon. For the five o'clock news."

"I'll bet."

She turned, pushing past Amy and Dave, and forcing him to follow her out. After her office, the lab was an island of sanity, with its gleaming walls and paneled ceiling and pleated ventilation ducts, the high-intensity lamps on wheeled stands, the rack of neatly hanging lab coats she never wore. The Objects Conservator and her assistant were quietly working on a ceramic statuette in the adjoining room. Her own new project, cleaning a trustee's Degas of a young ballerina, rested on the quilted tarp on the heat vacuum table in the center of the floor.

"A Degas?" He was playing to the crowd. "Not like that Schiele in our Brandt case. Right, Lily?"

Seated Female Nude with Raised Right Arm III, the Egon Schiele watercolor of an emaciated girl with her legs spread, flashed in her head. With it came a fury as bright and sharp as the scalpel in her tool drawer. Forgetting her audience, she wheeled on Paul. "You think you can waltz in here and pick up—"

He stepped back. "This has nothing to do with us. Just come with me to the crime scene."

"What for?"

"Your expertise. What Harry trained you for."

"Paul—"

Dave's eyes danced. "Who's Harry?"

"The man who made Lily so observant." His words were

playful; the riff wasn't. "Didn't you know she has a perfect eye?"

"Leave my dad out of this," she warned.

"Perfect?" Dave tugged at his forelock. "Shall I bow to you, Lily?"

"I mean it, Paul." The lab fell silent.

"Fine." He raised his hands in mock surrender, and she marched him to the door. "You've never seen Kurtz's private collection, have you?" he stage-whispered. "I hear he has two Sisleys and a Van Gogh."

"Using masterpieces as bait? That's disgusting!"

He stopped. She saw it in his eyes again—a new uncertainty.

"The crime scene's... unusual," he said. "You see things experts miss. Harry's game, right?"

Seeing wasn't just a game.

When she was a third-year lawyer, she'd been assigned to sell a rural bank. With the sale about to close, the senior partner complimented her on her documents, then asked if she'd bothered to visit the bank. *What for?* she said. *To make sure it's real,* he replied. The next day she drove fifty miles to the plains, met the bank's officers, and toured the facility. She was being hazed, but the lesson stuck: Life was more than data points. Later, when she saved Elena Brandt's gallery from ruin because she looked—and saw—that Egon Schiele watercolor for the fake it was, she got a glimmer of what her eye could do.

"Just an hour of your time, Lily," Paul was saying.

"I think I'll let you and the cops handle it."

But the museum obsessed over its message. What would the Talking Points on the murder of its chief benefactor be? Kurtz's fingerprints were everywhere you looked, from the Kurtz Building to the Kurtz Skybridge to his name on the wall next to countless pieces of art. And something more important than Talking Points was at stake: the visitors streaming in every day on the promise of being moved by art. When she entered a gallery, she felt the same hush, the anticipation of an orchestra tuning up. All those excited faces—would Kurtz's death overshadow the art, distract them from what the museum really had to offer?

She looked at Paul again. Despite his career achievements and bravado, was there a sadness tugging at his eyes? Something wasn't right. What harm was there in going to the crime scene and taking a look?

Chapter Three

Built by an oil baron's widow and bought by an Italian financier as a surprise gift for his wife, the Kurtz Castle had a two-story arched portico, stone parapets and a coat of arms filched from *Burke's Peerage*. Its wrought-iron doors, copper-framed windows, greenhouse and lily pond added charm, but the storybook effect was undercut by a Mobile Crime Unit van and a half-dozen police cars parked out front.

"I think you'll want this," Paul said. He held out his snowy hanky.

She shook her head. The last thing she wanted was to smell cloves.

He showed his ID to a uniformed officer at the gate. A plainclothes cop escorted them in. They went from an entrance hall with a travertine staircase with twisted railings and bronze plaques, through a living room with a carved marble fireplace, a walnut parquet floor, gold-plated light fixtures, and a Cezanne and a Picasso. A fan was running a few rooms away. At the soaring library paneled in red oak, the fairy tale ended.

The first thing she registered were the hot police lights and men in sport coats and ties talking quietly as they clustered around an object against the far wall. The second was the stench. Then the frigid air from a ventilation system on full blast and the loud whir of an industrial fan. Paul hadn't mentioned Kurtz's body would be there.

Something cool and crisp pressed into her hand. His hanky.

The talking had stopped, the men were watching her. She was glad she'd skipped breakfast. She balled up the hanky and slipped it in her pocket.

Propped on an upholstered chair against a wall papered in celadon silk with gold leaves, Kurtz stared imperiously. His head was intact, and his thinning silver hair was parted at the side and darkened and slicked with brilliantine. His hands rested on the chair's arms in a lord of the manor pose. From his chest down, he was riven in two. There was so much blood she couldn't tell if he was clothed, or even if he had skin. The Klieg lights flickered, creating a grotesque chiaroscuro. Paul seemed unaffected by the odor and gore. Maybe it was because he'd grown up on a farm.

"When was he found?" she asked.

"This morning, by his butler," a paunchy detective replied. He seemed to be in charge. She almost missed the wink to his colleagues. *Indulge the little lady so we can get this stiff outta here.*

Paul stepped in smoothly. "Ms. Sparks has been invaluable to the FBI. She's a pro like you."

Their faces spoke resentment, skepticism, and doubt. How did they feel being one-upped by a Fed in a fancy suit jetting in from D.C., and some blonde he was probably shacking up with? It must've been hard for him to come to her for help. She ran through her dad's training.

Prioritize.

Focus on one thing at a time.

Quantify, assign a value to each data point.

It's only what you refuse to see that can hurt you.

Details, please...

But nothing prepared her for this. She closed her eyes to block out the lights and faces and stench. *Think of it as a work of art, like the bird Jack caught.*

Specks of fluff by her night stand, a tiny red smear on the floor under her bed. The huddled mass fit neatly in her palm. Then the maggots.... Jack coolly watching, concealment versus credit resolved—*it took you long enough!* His jade cat-eyes devouring her with the naked passion of a lover. *I did it for you....*

"Lily?" Paul said.

"Can you turn off those lights?" The steadiness of her voice surprised her. "And the fan. They're distracting."

He signaled one of the men, and the heat and noise cut off. "Just your impressions," he said softly. "I'll send you the photos later."

Breathing through her nose, she approached the body. Kurtz's torso had skin, but every inch of it was flayed. She reached into her backpack for the tool of her trade.

"What the hell is that?" the detective asked.

"A loupe," Paul said admiringly. Every conservator worth her salt carried one.

She peered closer, trying to keep the nausea at bay. *Just another canvas.* Now she saw dozens, hundreds of geometric slashes and pointillist pricks, driven to the bone.

Artists control their conditions.

"Was he tied up?" she asked.

"Not that we can tell," the detective said.

"Were these wounds inflicted before he died?"

"Huh?"

Paul came to her rescue. "This took time," he explained. "The killer couldn't subdue Kurtz long enough to carve him up if he was conscious."

A whiff of excrement emanated from the wall. She took four steps back. Daubed like impasto on the celadon silk were gobbets of intestine. From the flaying, or added later? Some gobs appeared completely dry, others wet-on-wet. Did he tamp down Kurtz's guts with an instrument, then rub them in with his finger? They were confined to a specific area.

Nothing an artist does is accidental.

Putting away her loupe and stepping farther back, she turned to the composition. Art was deliberate, with an eye toward how it would be viewed. To the left of the chair was a divan with a coat and hat. If you ignored the divan, the tableau was compact, rectangular. The back of the chair created a strong horizontal line that tightened the structure. But was Kurtz meant to be viewed head-on? She moved back and forth, examining the scene from different angles.

Degas said the frame is the painting's pimp.

What was central to Kurtz's display, what was his proper

frame?

With the fan off, the smell had become a rancid, nauseating reek. The cops were getting impatient. They wanted to wrap it up, but she wasn't ready. She looked again at the pale green silk, the crimson daubs...

Aha!

The wall itself was part of the display. But something bothered her. She was missing an important detail. She refocused on the chair. Granted Kurtz's torso was split from sternum to hip, but something was unnatural about his legs. She took another six paces back, feeling the men behind her part to give her room.

"Why are his legs bent like that?"

"He was tall," the detective replied. Papers rustled. "Six-one."

"Were his ankles broken?"

"How'd you know that?" he demanded.

"They'd have to be, for his feet to curl like that under the chair.... An inside joke."

"Joke?"

Did I say that out loud? But painters inserted all sorts of things in a canvas or frame that had meaning only to them. "Maybe he wanted to make it look like the chair cut off Kurtz's legs."

"Huh?"

"Was anything stolen?" she asked.

"No," the detective said.

"Alarm triggered?"

"It and the cameras were disabled, but Kurtz's paintings are armed. That pissed the burglar off."

At that gala, how quickly Kurtz's flattery had turned to insolence! Did he insult his killer? She stepped back one last time. In the natural light, the wounds seemed artistic, impressionistic. But something about his legs...

—

The detective signaled the medical examiner to remove the body. Crime scene specialists bagged and tagged the remaining evidence. It was almost dark when she and Paul left. He put his arm around her and before she could stop her herself she leaned in.

"I owe you a drink," he said.

She pulled away. "Some other time."

"There's something I want—"

"Let's not go there, Paul."

He dropped his arm. "Come on, Lily. One drink doesn't mean a thing."

She hesitated. "I have a date."

He opened the passenger door and waited for her to buckle in. By the time he was behind the wheel, he was all business. It was better that way.

"Just between you and me, what did the crime scene tell you?" he asked.

"I felt like I was looking at a painting."

He stared like she was nuts. "You think an actual artist killed Kurtz?"

"Yes. And he cropped the body to fit the frame."

Chapter Four

Lily unpacked the Boston Market takeout. Barbequed ribs, sweet corn and...

"Look, Dad. Pecan pie!"

Harry Sparks never gained weight. In retirement he'd changed uniforms: a tan windbreaker and faded Rockies cap for the leather U. S. Postal Service bag and satin-striped trousers he'd worn for forty years. Like her, he was short and wiry, but there the resemblance ended. She got her hair and grey eyes from her mom; his were an unapologetic brown. Now, as they lit up at the food, she sighed with relief. After this godawful day, in the kitchen of her childhood home, with its worn linoleum and cupboards and the scarred table where he always sat, she was finally safe.

"Where's your food?" he said.

"I'm not hungry." Would she ever get Kurtz's stench out of her head?

"Oh." It wasn't his style to ask why. He dug into the ribs.

She brought dinner every week, his same favorites, dreading him losing his appetite. He didn't smoke or drink, and aside from puttering in the yard, watching baseball and playing penny poker, he had no hobbies. The red-roofed bungalow was a cave. And the neighborhood didn't help either: the working-class enclave on the east side of town had become Denver's pop-top capital, with SUVs and McMansions on every block. Where neighbors once gossiped comfortably over fences, no yards were left to fence.

"How's Jack?" he said. He liked cats.

"He passed his physical this morning."

"Still trying to please you, eh?" He knew about the bird.

"He's very... male."

"Well, if he wants to hang out with an old fart like me, bring 'im over."

A wave of affection swept her, and she rose and kissed him on the top of his head. His hair was thinning, that and a worsening limp from childhood polio his only signs of age. He squeezed her hand and returned to his barbequed ribs.

"How's work?" he said.

"Funny you should ask..."

"Yeah?"

"I got called in on a case."

"By your old firm?"

He'd been so proud when she worked her way through law school, graduated at the top of her class, and was recruited by a Seventeenth Street firm. For him, it wasn't the money. *You have to believe in something bigger than yourself, Lily, why not the law?* Her attention to detail quickly earned her kudos in the corporate department, where she shuffled piles of money around a desk. When Elena Brandt retained the firm to represent her gallery, they assigned the case to her. *Looted art? Put Sparks on it. No different from tracing a real estate title—she'll chase that rabbit down the hole!* The gallery case was her reprieve from a slow corporate death, but her downfall too. It was how she met Paul.

"No, Dad. It's an art thing."

"Oh." He tried to hide his disappointment. "But if they called you in, they know you're good."

She washed his plate and put the leftover ribs in the refrigerator, then rummaged through the freezer for the vanilla ice cream she'd brought last time. It was gone. *Good.* She warmed his pie in the microwave and watched him eat it. How many times had she tried to explain why she left law to become a conservator—that art, too, was bigger than herself? He'd taken her to museums, but he never understood. Because he'd taught her to look at paintings, but not to really see them?

Paul had opened her eyes to art and seeing him today brought it all back. *When you look at a painting, Lily, what do you feel?* A conservator became as intimate with a canvas as the artist himself. Sure, she had to understand the stroke and brushes and pigments the painter used, but more important were the emotions he sought to evoke. And some painterly surfaces begged to be touched. Unlike Gina, in the sanctity of her lab she could touch all she wanted. Kurtz's killer liked to touch too. Was Kurtz his canvas?

"I don't know what to do, Dad."

"With that case?"

"It's ... a police thing. The cops will handle it."

He looked up from his pie, more alert than in weeks. "Start at the beginning. Facts."

She sat again. "An FBI agent came to my office."

"Details, please."

"Six foot two, black hair, green eyes..." *I met him ten years ago and slept with him.*

"What did he want?" he said.

"To take me to a crime scene and tell him what I saw." *To break my heart again because he's still married.*

"And you went?"

"Yes." *I did, and he will.*

"What did you see?"

"The dead body of a bigwig from the museum." *That I'll never get over Paul.*

"Does he want you to help him some more?"

"Yes."

He threw up his hands. "Then what the hell's the problem?" He tried to soften it. "You know the drill, honey. The truth is facts, what you see with your own eyes. Look and follow wherever they go. Where would that little boy on the 1800 block of Gaylord be if I'd looked away? Who would *I* be?"

His first mail route was near Cheesman Park, where she now lived. He studied everything on his beat: dogs, newcomers, disrupted patterns. When he saw the boy's rubber ball in the same spot for three days, wet from the sprinkler, he told a cop. The cop investigated. The boy's father had broken his son's jaw. He was arrested for child abuse and her dad got a commendation. Years later the boy wrote thanking him. But couldn't he lay off her for once?

Being observant was his talent. Had he passed it on to make up for her losing her mom? A memory of a blonde woman at a door with a suitcase flickered in Lily's head. *Why won't she look at me?* As quickly as she came, she was gone. But here he was, still pushing.

"I'm not you, Dad."

"Of course you are! And you're tough." He reached across the table and brushed the bangs from her forehead, gently tracing the small white scar they concealed. "Remember that tree you fell out of, out back?"

She didn't, though he'd told the story a hundred times. Just as provenance was a painting's history—who owned it, when and where it was exhibited, the hands through which it passed—her provenance was her identity. Where and how she lived, the experiences and people that shaped her. When her dad was gone, that scar would be another piece of history lost.

"Don't count on anything but your eye, Lily. Who would you be without it?"

She brought his dessert plate to the sink and cranked up the faucet. Neither of them could stand self-pity. "Still playing poker with Walt?" The widower next door.

"His goddamn son put him in a nursing home."

She dried the plate and wiped her eyes with the towel. "Why?"

"So he could sell the damn house! They'll put up a monstrosity like that one on the corner."

She came up behind him and gently massaged his bony shoulders. "Want me to stay over? I'll make up the bed in my old room."

"Naw." He patted her hand. "You go home to Jack."

Chapter Five

The Kurtz Auditorium slowly filled with somber faces. Two dozen rows of plush red seats descended in a narrowing semicircle to a curved stage with a podium and cinema-sized video screen. From the screen, a twenty-foot George Kurtz glowered down at his final audience.

Taking her place in the third row, Lily watched the governor, the mayor, two congressmen and a senator file in, followed by the museum's major donors, docents and staff. She waved two rows back to Amy, in a black turtleneck instead of her usual snowy blouse with flowing sleeves. Next to her sat Dave. His concessions to the occasion were a tweed jacket, a white dress shirt with frayed cuffs, and a worn leather belt instead of suspenders. Nick had followed them in but stood against the wall, as if unsure whether his provisional status merited a seat.

The coverage of Kurtz's murder two days earlier had been surprisingly scant. In the sixty-second clip of the press conference on the evening news, the chief of police called it "an unfortunate death" but assured the public the perpetrator posed no threat. *The Denver Post* attributed to an unnamed source speculation that Kurtz surprised a burglar. There was no mention of FBI involvement. She skimmed the hastily assembled program that volunteers were distributing at the door. The cover featured the same glowering studio portrait of Kurtz. The only indication he was dead were the dates: 1938-2018.

Gina entered with Museum Director Michel Roland.

Michel waved and smiled at trustees and patrons, stopping to awkwardly squeeze the shoulder of an overweight woman in dark glasses in the front row. Who was she? Gina sat next to her, and he bounded up to the stage.

Everything about Michel suggested approachability: his snub nose and toothy grin, made more dazzling by enamel a touch too bright, the small eyes that disappeared into cracks of merriment when he laughed, even the slope-shouldered European tailoring of his suits. Hiring him from the Louvre had been a coup after his tiff with a critic who questioned a Da Vinci's authenticity. Insisting the eye is king and refusing to subject the Old Master to scientific tests had won Michel admirers, and he was the engine behind the museum's highly successful Christian Dior exhibit. But beneath his brio and bonhomie lay an iron fist and a Gallic contempt for Americans. Begging for sponsorships and gifts was so… un-French.

The lights dimmed. Michel delicately cleared his throat and lowered the mic. "We are here to honor the life of our beloved patron, George Kurtz."

The scowling face on screen was replaced by a sullen boy on horseback.

"George grew up on a Colorado ranch. His father, George Sr., was a titan of the oil fields who broadened his empire to cattle and mining. Some might call young George's childhood privileged, even glamorous…"

Cue a stony-faced teen in jodhpurs, holding a polo mallet.

"…but at age fifteen he left the comforts of the ranch for the untamed wilds of the East." Michel chuckled at his little joke. The polo player was replaced by a phalanx of boys in grey uniforms in front of a brick building with an American flag.

"George, Jr. excelled at boarding school, then earned a petroleum engineering degree…Oh, what's this?"

Kurtz kneeling with a rifle and a bloodhound.

"His daughter Angela—" Michel waved impishly at the dumpy woman in the front row—"must have slipped this in." He glanced at his notes. The photo montage was hastily assembled, but he himself never improvised. "Who's that, Angela? Your dad's favorite hunting dog, Gus?"

Angela nodded, and Gina patted her on the back. Angela pulled away.

Michel returned to his script. "George, Jr. transformed his father's company into the largest privately held oil and gas operation in the world. He believed fiercely in the free market, but at heart he was a philanthropist, never more generous than he was to the museum."

No need to remind donors how vital they were to a museum with no endowment; the plush red seats they sat in were marked by row and number so the auditorium could be rented out for events. Nor did Michel need to mention how Kurtz died, or even that he was dead. He stuck to his Talking Points.

Highlights of Kurtz's public life paraded across the screen, shot after shot of him at museum functions, holding a wine glass and hobnobbing with Michel and Gina. A quick one of him with daughter Angela that was out of focus and out of place. His retreats in Aspen and Palm Springs, presiding at a symposium in Jackson Hole… The montage was fit for a Hollywood movie. Was Michel in denial over Kurtz's gruesome death? Or a magician, flattering his patrons by reminding them of their exclusivity while he distracted them from why they were there? Attention wandering, Lily glanced around the auditorium.

Paul was standing next to Nick. Didn't the FBI have local agents? Kurtz was getting the VIP treatment, and though Paul had asked her for scuttlebutt, he'd be going back to D.C. as soon as this dog-and-pony show was over. Back to whatever was missing… He'd pooh-poohed the killer being an artist, but what if the museum was involved? If she were looking for Kurtz's murderer, she'd start right here.

The first rule is assume nothing.

Cats knew one wrong assumption could be their last. Jack had a protocol for assessing strangers: he appraised size, shape, and how the person moved before slowly approaching to sniff out identity and intent. He knew appearances were deceiving—if only she'd been so smart about Paul! He was looking at the front row, where Gina coyly adjusted the neckline of her dress. Did she know he was watching her? Of course. A guy like him would probably—

Avoid subjectivity.

Nick. Wavy auburn hair, intense blue eyes, good-looking in a nerdy way. More than just a little attractive; a couple of times he'd looked like he wanted to ask her out. Now he stared at the screen with the jittery fascination of someone watching his own life unfold.

Stick to what you can see.

Nick had tapered fingers and no wedding ring. He also had an eye for art. During lectures he took notes and asked good questions about materials and technique. He'd bailed her out the other day on the sewage field in *Seven*, and it was sharp of him to notice that the man in the painting wasn't carrying threshing tools. She'd looked up his address. He lived two blocks from her, in a house near Cheesman Park. If he had a wife, at least he didn't hide her halfway across the country.

Quantify intangibles.

Angela Kurtz appeared to be in her mid-thirties. Unless she was blind, the Jackie Onassis shades were way too dark for an auditorium and too small for her heavy face. Her black crepe dress was more than Lily could afford, but a size too large. Was she losing weight? She'd shifted in her seat to be as far as possible from Gina.

Lily looked over her shoulder again at Paul. She still had his hanky. She had to launder it and give it back—

Focus, dammit.

Angela fiddled with the clip in her somewhat disheveled hair. Like her shades, the clip was too small for the job; unlike her dress, it looked like it came from a drugstore. The nails on the fingers fiddling with the clasp were polished but bitten to the quick, the cuticles ragged. Her watch hung loosely on her wrist. Granted, she was mourning her murdered father. But did the weight loss and schizoid grooming suggest a transition that began before he died?

"Kurtz, Sr. was chairman of the state Republican Party," Michel was saying. "Son George eschewed politics, embracing bipartisan and social causes. He endowed a chair in Law and Economics at the University of Colorado School of Law…"

A law school publicity shot with the dean.

"... and championed the rights of our least fortunate with grants to the ACLU and National Association of Criminal Defense Lawyers in support of federal sentencing reform."

Kurtz shaking the hand of a woman in a power suit on the steps of the U.S. Capitol while a bespectacled and bemused head of the NACDL looked on. The photo lingered on the screen, as if to engrave the memory of Kurtz's beneficence in the minds of his fellow patrons forever.

"We close with thanks to our beloved benefactor, and our promise to assist his cherished Angela in continuing his good works."

The lights came up and mourners began filing out. Gina murmured something to Angela, who ignored her. Blushing, Gina turned away. She reached for her purse and Lily came face to face with her. Gina blinked rapidly, then smoothly regained her poise.

"Who's that man?" She was looking at Paul.

"Who?"

"The one standing over there."

"Nick?"

"Nice try, Lily. He was in your lab yesterday." She had spies everywhere. "You left together and didn't return."

"Oh! You mean Paul."

"Paul?"

"Riley." He was leaning on the wall like a cat in the sun. "An FBI agent looking into Kurtz's case."

"Is he married?"

Lily smiled like Jack when she opened a can of tuna. "How would I know?"

"Stay away from him," Gina ordered. "And Angela Kurtz too."

"Why?"

"Crime is not in the museum's best interests."

"How reassuring."

"Take it as a friendly warning, Lily." She gestured to the podium, where Michel was accepting congratulations and condolences. "Straight from the top."

Chapter Six

Sun flooded in from the skylight of the Brown Palace Hotel. Shaded lamps welcomed aging eyes, and a harp softly played. Conservatively dressed in her trademark oversized red-framed glasses, off-the-shoulder cashmere sweater, and shantung silk trousers, Elena Brandt helped herself to a scone. An armload of vintage black Bakelite bangles completed her fashion statement. Their monthly high tea was the only occasion for which Lily dressed up, wearing her knee-skimming pencil skirt, retro-chic sweater set, and ballet flats in deference to the proprietress of Brandt Gallery of Fine Arts. Elena would have said the debt ran the other way.

"Tea, dear?" she said.

As if summoned by the tug of an invisible cord, a black-vested waiter silently appeared with a silver pot of jasmine tea. Elena did it by sheer force of presence; now in her eighties, she'd lived a lifetime of dealing with servants and flunkies and had suffered a few knocks along the way. The art world was no place for amateurs or fools. They waited as the server poured their tea into bone china cups before gliding away.

"You're looking a bit peaked." Elena knew her too well.

"Things have been a little hectic." Lily took a sip. "How's business?"

"The auctions were disappointing, but I have my sources." By sources Elena meant the private collectors whose identities would accompany her to her grave. A painting might have belonged to "an English private collection" or "a

Russian noble family." The dealer knew better than to ask. Even prices were recorded on the books in code.

Bangles clinking softly, Elena broke off a corner of her scone and daintily placed it in her mouth. Her face was a nest of wrinkles and her white hair short enough for the Marines, but her smile was as guileless and fresh as a girl's. Now her sharp eyes appraised Lily. "What's new at the museum? I hope you're not regretting your decision."

Elena had encouraged her to return to school for a degree in art conservation. It took three scholarships, her entire savings, and eight years to get where she was. Night courses in undergraduate chemistry, technical drawing at the Art Students League, two years for the Masters in Painting Conservation at NYU, an internship at the Smithsonian's Hirschhorn Museum in D.C. and a Mellon Fellowship at the National Gallery, then four more years at the DeYoung in San Francisco. When the position finally opened in Denver, she booked the first flight home. Her dad was overjoyed to have her for more than holidays and the occasional weekend, and she was glad she'd sublet the condo she'd bought while she was at the law firm. She never could have afforded it now.

"No regrets," she said. "Conservation is a noble profession."

Elena laughed. Both knew that meant it didn't pay much. "Then what's wrong, dear?"

"George Kurtz was murdered."

Elena took a sip of tea, and grimaced because it was too hot. "So I heard."

"You don't sound too broken up."

"If you'd known George, you wouldn't be either…"

Lily took a finger sandwich from the middle tray. Egg salad, which she didn't particularly like, but this way Elena would continue.

"He didn't use my gallery. He bought only though his agent, Morley Sullivan. Sully got tips."

The art world ran on speed, secrecy, and greed. Every collector wanted to beat the competition, and an agent who could sniff out masterpieces like truffles was priceless. But ego and pride blinded collectors, and in a world where perception was more important than truth, even experts could be deceived. Did Elena's antipathy for Kurtz go deeper than being snubbed?

"Why didn't you like him?" Lily asked.

"George was cruel. His father was a macho ass; he and his wife toured Europe and sent him to a military academy. After he took over the business, George treated his employees miserably and his wives even worse."

"Yet he was a philanthropist…"

"Philanthropy is about power, Lily. The question is how you wield it."

"He was certainly generous to the museum."

"You think George loved art?" Elena laughed scornfully. "Nobody questions a benefactor."

As the harpist strummed on, Lily slowly chewed. She wasn't buying it. For one thing, there was the sheer scale of Kurtz's donations. And what about his contributions to the NACDL and the ACLU?

"Do you know his daughter?"

"Angela?" Elena scoffed. "Now *there's* a suspect."

"She seemed upset at his memorial."

"The way George pitted her against her brother, she should be relieved." Elena lowered her voice confidentially. "The boy committed suicide, you know." She helped herself to a round topped with smoked salmon mousse and capers. "Angela packed on the pounds after that. But inheriting all that money was probably worth it."

Kurtz's daughter dancing on his grave? Grieving or not, there'd been something touching about her the other day. But Elena was being uncharacteristically cagy.

"Who hated him most?" Lily said.

"Besides his exes and mistresses, one of whom you know?"

Lily leaned forward. "Who?"

"Your esteemed Curator of Paintings."

"Gina Wheelock?"

"How do you think the museum got that Caillebotte?"

She remembered Kurtz's clammy touch at the gala, his fingernails buffed and sharp. Those same hands clutching the armchair in his library, the tendons contracting to claws. If Elena's gossip was true, she pitied Gina. But could she really be a suspect? That seemed as absurd as Elena's portrait of Angela. She tried again.

"Who was Kurtz's worst enemy?"

"The Department of Justice. He was facing a dozen indictments."

"The DOJ doesn't prosecute executives."

Elena shrugged. "I told you, dear. I have sources."

Lily set down her sandwich. "Do you think the killer could be an artist?"

"An artist?" Elena laughed. "The ones I know take out their aggressions on a canvas, with a paintbrush or palette knife. Why do you ask?"

"Just curious."

The waiter brought fresh plates. Elena selected a chocolate truffle. "Delicious... Not hungry?" Her shrewd eyes missed nothing. "You haven't said what's really going on."

"An FBI agent came to my office."

"Aha! The one you slept with on the gallery case? Paul something..."

Lily sighed. "Ancient history."

"I thought that was a mistake."

"Yeah, it was. Married men—"

"Not your affair. Breaking up." Elena took another chocolate. "I saw the two of you fight over that Schiele. You set the room on fire."

Seated Nude was a watercolor gouache of a red-haired girl outlined in black crayon on tinted paper. The model was Schiele's sister, Gerti. Gerti sprawled in the chair with her legs spread and her right hand cupping her ear. An awkward pose, but that arm created tension, a taut energy that ran to Gerti's nipples. The left arm's line broke above the elbow, softened with the curve of Gerti's hip, and ended at the hand resting on her scarlet vulva. *Look away*, she taunted Lily, *if you dare*.

The Nazis banned Schiele's work as degenerate art. *Seated Nude* passed from his nephew to a Jewish dealer in Vienna, then disappeared until it resurfaced eighty years later in an attic in Zagreb. How it got there was a mystery, but a century after Schiele died, he was hot. When Elena acquired the watercolor from a New York gallery to great fanfare, the dealer's heirs hired a looted art expert and sued for its return in federal court. With her gallery, her reputation, and all she owned on the line, she hired Lily's firm.

The FBI sent Paul to Denver. His brashness back then was real, and because they were adversaries, whatever he discovered Lily made it her business to disprove. Days hunched over files spilled to debates about art over drinks. With the clock ticking down, they flew together to Vienna and Zagreb to interview witnesses, search archives, and visit museums. He was trained in art history through his work, but this was the first time she'd truly grasped paintings. It cracked open her universe. *Look for the randomness, Lily, the imperfection that lets the painting breathe....* The eroticism of Schiele's portraits, and his touches of ultramarine and cobalt and rose madder, left her breathless—alive. But back home, she was forced to accept the truth: *Seated Nude* belonged to the dealer's heirs. The night before the trial, she and Paul sat across from each other in her firm's glassed-in conference room. The table was littered with yellow pads and art books. From the center Gerti stared up, issuing her dare.

"It's here, Paul. I know it is."

He folded his arms and leaned back. Across the street skyscrapers were lighting up; outside the conference room, elevators pinged as lawyers and paralegals left for the night. "Get some sleep. Tomorrow's a big day."

"Schiele liked emaciated models. See the hint of fleshiness in her thigh?"

"That again?"

For the hundredth time, she pored through Schiele's catalogue raisonné, the compendium of his known works. And suddenly she had it. She reached for a pencil.

He yawned. "Are we waiting for the cleaning crew?"

"He used broken contours, Paul. He started at her neck and drew without looking at his paper. He lifted his pencil when he wanted to capture the light."

"I'll spring for Thai—"

"Picture her at the end of this table, lit from behind."

"Or a nice bloody steak."

Staring at Gerti at the end of the table, and with pencil poised in the air above *Seated Nude*, she traced Schiele's line from the neck down. The right arm was fine. On the left she came to a halt.

"What now?" he said. But he rose and came to her side.

She looked down at *Seated Nude*. In the watercolor, the left arm's line broke near the elbow, like she remembered. Now visualizing the light coming from the side, she retraced that line in the air again. Something was wrong; instead of breaking at the elbow, the watercolor's line should have broken on the shoulder. She did it a third time. Whatever direction the light came from, breaking at the elbow made no sense. Paul had talked about imperfection, the space for a painting to breathe, but— The scent of clove caressed her cheek. She turned. "Do you see—"

He closed his hand over hers and traced. He did it twice more.

"Shit," he said softly. "The wrong imperfection." Then he turned and kissed her. She didn't remember who shut the blinds or swept away the books and pads, but she remembered everything else. Their first time was on that conference room table. Every detail was emblazoned in her head.... *I want that again.*

"He wouldn't have anything to do with your interest in Kurtz?" Elena said now.

"What? No, it's the museum—"

"George Kurtz isn't a watercolor. You think solving his murder will win Paul back?"

"Of course not!"

"You've had no other relationships in ten years, dear. Why do you think that is?"

"I—"

"Don't let him go again, Lily."

She stared into her teacup. "He lied to me."

"Did he really, dear?"

The dealer's heirs had dropped their suit, and Elena sold *Seated Nude* as a fake to a Los Angeles media mogul who called it one of the best Schieles he'd ever seen. But Lily remembered Paul jetting back and forth to D.C. as the case wrapped up, those nights at her condo, the calls and texts he went to the bathroom to answer. He never said they were FBI business and she never asked. When she finally confronted him, he didn't pretend his marriage was on the rocks. She blamed herself; it was right in front of her, and she didn't see it. The Brandt case made her the toast of her firm, but every time she walked past that conference room she wanted to scream or hurl a brick through the glass. The day before she was to make partner, she resigned.

"You think you're the only girl to love a married man?" Elena said.

She looked up. Her mentor never discussed her past.

"I did it twice," Elena continued. "Broke up three marriages, including my own. One was an artist, the other— What does it matter? Let's just say I was bored and stupid."

"I'm not that girl anymore."

Elena shook her head. "If you love that FBI agent, don't be a fool."

———

Office towers twinkled in an indigo sky. Waiting at Elway's bar, Lily checked her lipstick in her compact. Pomegranate—the soft overhead light gave the red an undertone of pink, as if she'd bitten into ripe seeds. The woman in the mirror stared enigmatically back. Paul had suggested meeting at the swank steakhouse because it was near his hotel, but he didn't say they shared a lobby. And since when did the Feds spring for the Ritz-Carlton?

"Such a tiny mirror." He'd come up behind her.

The compact was small and slim, with a swirling galaxy embossed in gold on the lid and tiny crystal stars. "It was my mother's." She snapped it shut and returned it to her makeup bag. "You must be on a hell of an expense account."

"This case is a priority."

"I'll try to make your time worth it."

The maître d' seated them, and the waiter came over.

"Gin martini up, super cold, just wave the bottle of vermouth over it," Paul ordered without asking. "Two olives."

What else does he remember?

"Do you keep Pappy?" Paul said. "The 25?"

It used to be Jim Beam.

"Yes, sir. Neat?"

Who does he drink 25-year-old bourbon with now?

The waiter left, and Paul turned to business. "What did you find out?"

"Kurtz had enemies," she said.

"Who?"

"The DOJ and lots of women."

He smiled indulgently. "Anyone I know?"

"That depends."

"Gina Wheelock doesn't have the strength to cut off a man at the knees—"

"Unlike me?"

"—and Angela Kurtz is too out of shape."

The waiter brought their drinks.

"Your turn," she said. "Any leads on the weapon?"

"There were two. One metal, the other wood with a sharp point. They found splinters in the wounds."

She sipped her martini. "What else?"

"You were right, Kurtz's killer disabled him first. The preliminary report says he used methane gas."

Meeting him here was a mistake. Her martini was hitting fast and his eyes were devouring her. In two minutes they could be in his room.

"The *Post* called it a burglary," she said.

He shrugged. "A sophisticated ring's been working the Country Club area. They've kept it quiet, but the cops think there's an inside guy at an alarm company."

Back to business. This was more like it. The urge to kiss him had passed, but what happened to the rest of her martini? "Since when does a burglar subdue a homeowner with gas, Paul? Look into Kurtz's finances."

"Finances?" He waved dismissively. His hands were strong and square, the nails trimmed, not buffed—no trace of that farm boy now. The Rolex on his wrist confirmed he was climbing the FBI's ranks. "They think the killer knew someone on Kurtz's staff."

"Maybe he stiffed the wrong guy." It came out a little slurred. He'd ordered a second round. This one tasted stronger. "What else did the autopsy say?"

He tapped at papers inside his suitcoat; unlike Michel, he didn't need notes. "I'll send you the report." Was he amused?

"Tell me now."

"The wounds contained fibers from Kurtz's shirt, and traces of formaldehyde, hydroquinone and phthalates." His diction was clipped, the syllables precise.

"How well do you know Gina?" she said.

He set down his bourbon. "Maybe we should order."

"I'm not hungry."

"I can see that."

Her cheeks burned. "You did this to me."

"What?" He looked startled.

Opened my eyes, and I can't go back.

"What do you need me for, Paul?"

He stared at her, his expression unreadable.

This is crazy, he probably has kids!

"I'm driving you home," he said.

She shook her head and carefully rose. As steadily as she could, she left the restaurant. In the Prius, she checked her lipstick again and pulled out her cell. There was only one way to exorcise him. She scrolled down the museum directory and paused just a second before dialing.

"Nick?"

Chapter Seven

"What's that?" Amy said.

Lily hunched over her computer. How many drinks did she have with Nick? And that was before his athletic performance. She reached in her desk for three Advil and swallowed them dry.

What the hell was I thinking?

"Lily?" Amy said.

She looked back at the screen. Paul had e-mailed the autopsy report and crime scene photos. Except for the body, nothing in Kurtz's library was in disarray. The hat and coat were on the divan, as if their owner had just tossed them there. Temples throbbing, she zoomed in on the chair.

"Are those—legs?" Amy said.

"Don't look, child!" Dave stepped between Amy and the computer.

Lily didn't mind Dave traipsing in and out of the lab. She enjoyed his sly wit, he'd been around long enough to speak his mind, and tour groups requested him by name. Plus, he doted on Amy. He'd brought her a carrot juice and her favorite salad from Mad Greens across the plaza: craisins, pecans, and pears. He did that at least once a week.

Peering at the monitor, he whistled between his teeth. "Nice job."

"What do you see?" she asked.

"It's... experimental."

"I thought so, too."

She clicked to a photo of intestines on the wall.

"That's genius," he said. "Impasto Bolognese, anyone?"

"Dave!" Amy said.

"Sorry, Amy," he murmured.

"Don't worry," she told Amy. "The killer knocked him out with gas."

But she couldn't stop seeing Kurtz in that chair. Geometric slashes and pointillist pricks, intestines dabbed on a green silk wall patterned with leaves. What did they remind her of? She shook her head. There was something she'd been meaning to talk to Dave about.

"I saw your letter to the editor in *The Cherry Creek Chronicle*," she said. After a hedge fund acquired the *Post*, the monthly freebie was the only rag that really covered local news.

"The one about developers in bed with the City Council?" he said.

"Those mooch hacks should be recalled."

He shrugged modestly. "It's the proper thing to do."

"You play penny poker?"

He grinned. "My favorite sport!"

"There's somebody I want you to meet—"

A loud clearing of the throat interrupted them. Someone with a sinus infection? Gina Wheelock stood in the doorway.

"Gina, what a surprise!" The museum's administrative offices were in a separate building, and it was a relief not to have her and Michel breathing down her neck. Lily gestured discreetly to Amy to leave and take Dave with her. "I've been meaning—"

"What's on your computer?" Gina demanded.

She quickly exited the screen. "Nothing."

"I warned you to stay away from that FBI agent."

She has spies at Elway's?

"You mean Paul Riley?"

"Don't play dumb."

"There's nothing between us, Gina. But I'd like to talk about something." *A matter of professional distance.* "The other day I noticed you standing a little close to *Seven*."

"The rule is twelve inches," Gina said frostily.

Used to be eighteen, but we both know what a difference the right six inches make.

"I know, Gina, but trainees are awfully impressionable."
Gina smirked. "You've certainly impressed one of them."
She knows about Nick?

"Michel expects you to focus on your work," Gina
continued. "He has nothing but the greatest respect for your
eye...."

So long as it didn't challenge his. Shortly after he hired
Lily, he'd made that clear. She was cleaning a portrait for
a trustee when she noticed what appeared to be ink in the
craquelure, the lines that developed when paint shrank with
age. She took her suspicions to Michel. *Impossible,* he insisted,
the provenance is impeccable! The portrait's, or the trustee's?
He'd smiled coldly. *I hired you despite the Schiele, not because of
it.*

"...what you do best," Gina was saying. "But I'm not here
to lecture you. I want to borrow Amy later."

"Like a library book, or a chit to trade to the Louvre?"
Her headache was back, and she couldn't resist the jibe. Since
Kurtz donated *Seven,* Gina had been on more than just the
curatorial prowl. Was she trying to poach Amy?

"She's expressed an interest in an exhibition I want to
mount."

Don't think of her on top of Paul.

"How exciting! What sort of exhibit might that be?"

"Now, now..." Gina wagged her finger.

Amy did seem itchy lately. A day or two away from the
lab would be good for her.

"She's yours."

———

"Kids," Margo Hennessy muttered that evening as she
texted on her phone at the Cherry Creek bistro. "Who's the
new guy, Lily?"

She and Margo had started at the Seventeenth Street firm
on the same day. As its genteel white-shoe veneer rapidly
dissolved into sink-or-swim, they'd kept each other afloat.
They toasted victories, cried on each other's shoulders,
and traded tips on partners to avoid. Margo made partner,
married the guy she'd dated since college, and had two kids.
Now her CPA-husband kept house and her wardrobe cost

more than Lily earned in a year. But their friendship had endured, and once a month they caught up over dinner.

"What makes you think I had sex?"

"One: You're hung over, and you never drink alone. Two: You're forking that linguine like a lumberjack. Three: You look like a cat who swallowed a canary."

Lily winced at the memory of last night. "He's a docent trainee."

"You're too young to be a cougar, and aren't docents old?"

"He's thirty-two." And a lot more experienced than he looked.

"Jailbait!" Margo cried.

"All he's got in his refrigerator is beer. We're taking it slow." Not on the strength of last night, but at least she wasn't thinking about Paul every frigging minute. And this dinner had another agenda. "What can you tell me about George Kurtz?"

Margo's cell buzzed. She rolled her eyes. "I said give them macaroni," she hissed into the phone. "Of course they'll eat it. It's the only thing they eat!"

Lily smiled sympathetically, but her own biological clock was ticking. Thirty-six and what did she have to show for it? Margo had a partnership, a husband, and two angelic kids she seldom saw. Elena had a gallery and independence. She had a condo and a cat and zero job security. The Met in New York had a $3 billion endowment, and it was laying off staff. Her long-running war with Gina didn't help—as Amy liked to remind her.

Margo ended her call. "Mr. Wonderful is back on the hunt. You broke his heart."

Lily set down her fork. She didn't need to be reminded of what a mess she'd been after Paul. Her fling with the head of Litigation was worse: not just one married man, but two. "Can we get to Kurtz?"

Margo winked. "Off the record, right?"

"Always."

"We're representing his estate." Kurtz was a long-time client of the firm's. "It's a total rat-fuck with daughter Angela."

"How so?"

"A humongous trust and a daisy-chain of 501(c)s."

501(c)s were tax-exempt charitable foundations whose donors' identities were known only to the IRS. For deductions and anonymity, each year they were required to give five percent of their assets to nonprofits and refrain from lobbying and electoral politics. But rules kept law firms like theirs in business; with smart lawyers and an agency only too willing to look the other way, a 501(c)(3) educational organization could make a grant to a (c)(6) trade association, and by the time the money made its way to a think tank or a senator's war chest, it was untraceable.

"Any reason for the FBI to get involved?" Lily said.

"Why?" Margo asked suspiciously.

Lily shook her head. If she told her Paul was back on the scene, she could only imagine what her friend would say. "Where does Angela come in?"

Margo leaned forward. The restaurant was noisy, but this was privileged. "A fight over control of the trust. We warned Kurtz to be more specific in the documents, but masters of the universe never think they'll die. Between his daughter and his exes, it's a mess."

"Was he facing an indictment?"

Margo threw up her hands in mock innocence. "You didn't hear it from me."

"What was he indicted for?"

"Like I said, I don't know." Margo peered into her wine glass. "You know the Feds. They'd slap Kurtz on the wrist even if they had him dead to rights, and he's no Jean Valjean." They ordered chocolate lava cake and two spoons.

"Any other dirt?" Lily said.

"Kurtz was being sued over a company he bought. It's gone scorched earth and Mr. Wonderful's in charge." Margo looked at her mischievously. "I'm sure he'd let you pump him for details."

"Nothing's worth that."

They split the lava cake and the check.

———

Driving home, she thought about what Margo said. Was Kurtz's generosity to the museum a cover, to burnish his reputation while he funneled assets to less savory beneficiaries?

Elena, too had hinted at the 501(c) angle, and Angela Kurtz intrigued her. Less than a week had passed since her father's murder. Too late to drop her a note?

Resisting the temptation to swing past Nick's, she pulled into the underground parking garage at her condo. The fifteen-story concrete high-rise wasn't much from the outside, but it was close to downtown and the views were priceless. She'd begun renting when she was a young law firm associate and bought when the building went condo.

Overlooking Cheesman Park, the condo was surprisingly quiet and secure. Her two-bedroom on the tenth floor towered over majestic spruces, and the wraparound balcony had an unobstructed view of the Botanic Gardens. She'd have morning coffee there, and gaze down on the Japanese garden's freshly raked contours in the sand. In the evening she often grilled fish on the hibachi as she watched the shadows of mugo pines blacken in the lake. The balcony was Jack's favorite spot, too. She left the sliding door open a crack so he could slip in and out, sunning himself on the cement and finding secret places among her potted roses and tomato plants. Even after he killed the bird, she didn't have the heart to shut him in.

As soon as she turned her key in the lock, she knew something was wrong.

"Jack?" He always waited at the door.

She stood completely still, listening in the darkness. When she was sure she was alone, she flicked on the light. Nothing looked out of place, but she left the front door open.

Prioritize.

"Jack?" she called again.

No answer. The sliding door to her balcony was closed. She went to her bedroom and peered under the bed. No Jack.

What's different from before?

Kitchen counter gleaming, faucets turned all the way off. Hangers in her closet perfectly aligned. The clothes in her laundry basket—she'd been in such a rush to get to work that morning after her night with Nick, she couldn't possibly have been so neat. The intruder had tidied up after her.

Concentrate on details that don't stand out.

Desk even cleaner than she'd left it, pencil mug two inches farther from her computer than she comfortably reached. Dresser drawers and lingerie meticulously rifled, not pawed. None of it taken. Vials in her medicine chest lined up with labels facing out. A subtle rebuke for her minute sloppiness? Or was the intruder testing her eye?

Her birth control pills were missing. Not subtle at all. Was there something else he wanted her to find?

The only item in the waste basket was her toothbrush. Its bristles were splayed and matted, as if the intruder had scrubbed them against a hard surface. *Details, please.* Some were crossed over each other, like grass flattened by the wind.

She started to dial 911. Then she heard a sound. Claws scrabbling, an outraged *mew*? The broom closet in the back hall.

"Jack!"

He'd been the scrawniest kitten at the shelter, with a body and legs that were impossibly long and a tail that stopped an inch past where it should have ended. In the year since, he'd put muscle on his shoulders, and his short coat—a pelt, really—had become buttery soft. Now his fur was matted and acrid. He'd peed on himself, the ultimate insult to his dignity, and trembled as she held him to her chest. When his heart slowed, she set him down and reached again for her phone.

"Lily?" came a voice from the front doorway. "Is that you, dear?"

Her widowed neighbor, Louise, stood there in slippers and a robe. Louise of the molded salads and Coca Cola-braised pot roast. Louise who took in her mail and fed Jack when she was out of town. It was all she could do not to hug her.

"I thought I heard you," Louise said. "Everything all right?"

"Somebody broke in."

The only crime at the building had been years earlier, when a burglar scaled the exterior wall and made it to the sixth floor. Entering through balconies, he'd stolen jewelry and cash. Not birth control pills. And that toothbrush... The condo's walls were paper thin. When Paul had spent the night, they'd put on music; now she fell asleep to the sound of Louise's TV.

"Did you see or hear anything, Louise?"

"Just that gentleman friend of yours."

"Who?" She'd brought Mr. Wonderful home once. Or was it twice?

"Not the older man with the hair plugs from your law firm, dear. This was the handsome one, with the eyes that never blink."

Did Paul keep a key?

"It was around six," Louise said. "I was taking out my trash and he was standing at your door."

"Did he say anything?"

"Just waved. I do hope you don't chase him away again."

Chapter Eight

Degas's ballerina limbered up at the barre. Sensuous but innocent, she extended one satin-clad foot behind her. Light was represented by color and tone; it couldn't be reproduced. Her toe slippers gleamed.

"Where's the light coming from?" Lily asked Amy.

"The left."

The dancer's shadow projected onto the wall to her right, echoed by a softer shadow from her extended foot onto the floor. Degas mixed his paints with turpentine to achieve a matte, velvety effect. He never used varnish; he was opposed to its artifice, and the hard film into which it dried inevitably affected tone. Tone was more than contrast. The interplay of dark and light created structure, guiding the viewer's eye into the painting.

How Degas felt, however, was of no significance to the ballerina's current owner. Did he varnish this sublime creature to protect her from dust? But dust on an unvarnished irregular surface wasn't nearly as great a problem as dirt on a varnished one. The ballerina now wore a resinous brown coat.

"Varnish?" Amy asked.

"And nicotine. Our dancer lived with a chain smoker."

Lily touched the canvas gently, mindful of her oath: *First do no harm*. Surgeons buried their mistakes; conservators hung them on the wall. Early in her career, she'd exorcised any vestige of a cavalier nature. Now she never picked anything up without first assessing how it was constructed and should be handled. The ballerina was especially dear because without being sentimental, Degas had captured a girl on the cusp of womanhood. What female could forget the first time a stranger looked at her with desire, how confused and powerful and alive it made her feel?

"What's our first step, boss?" Amy said.

"Look. Then look some more."

Amy set up two wheeled lamps, one on each side of the ballerina. On the raised, textured surface of the canvas, the varnish caught the light unevenly. The erratic points of luster destroyed the matte effect and flattened the tone, making it difficult for the viewer to enter the painting.

"Lily?" Paul stood at her elbow with an overnight bag. After he rifled through her condo, she knew he'd show up. "I left three messages. One last night and two this morning."

"What do you want?"

"To talk."

"We're doing that now." She ran her loupe over the ballerina's tutu. When Degas painted it, were the tulle folds gold—or pink?

"Can we go to your office?" he said.

"Anything you have to say can be said here."

His neck flushed, and his hand crept to the back of it. Amy sidled away, but not too far.

Lily lowered her voice. "Why were you at my condo last night?"

"I wanted to take you to dinner."

"And when you didn't find me, you let yourself in."

"What?"

He's such a bullshitter I almost believe him.

The lab hummed with colleagues engrossed in their work. Across the floor the white-gloved Objects Conservator gingerly examined a porcelain figurine while her assistant worked on a bronze statuette with a mottled patina. The Degas ballerina waited.

"Why did you do that to my toothbrush?" she demanded. Stealing her birth control pills was such a cheap shot it wasn't even worth mentioning.

"What?" he repeated.

"And you didn't have to scare Jack!"

The flush crept to his face. "Who the hell is Jack?"

"Don't pretend."

"You were with Nick," he said.

Is he spying on me? "You're jealous of a provisional docent?"

"Provisional?" he snorted. "Poor guy hasn't proven himself to you yet?"

With as much dignity as she could muster, she went to her office. He closed the door behind them and stood across from her desk.

"I'm going back to D.C.," he said.

Ten years ago, all over again.

"The case is solved," he continued. "They're making an arrest."

She went to the window. A spring storm was blowing in from the west. The clouds looked like snow. He'd better get to the airport fast.

"Don't you want to know who killed Kurtz?" he said.

She didn't reply.

"It was a burglar after all. High on crack and caught red-handed in a house two blocks from Kurtz's. He has a record—"

She turned. "You believe that? Or is it an easy way back to D.C.?"

He stared. "You wanted me to go. Then and now." She turned away again. But he wasn't finished. "That's how you stay safe, isn't it?"

"No woman's safe—"

"You never let anyone in but your father. That guilty old—"

"At least he stayed. And he didn't screw around on his wife!"

For a long moment Paul was silent. When he spoke, it was with a new coldness. "To set the record straight, Lily, you threw me out. For two years I—"

"You—"

"No, you listen to me. You hide in a world of make-believe. You traded your law firm for this museum, but it's no sanctuary either. You're just like Harry, pretending it's all objectivity and facts. I pity you. Life isn't black and white.

But you're too perfect to see that." He straightened his tie and reached for his bag.

"And you're too stubborn and blind to see the killer's an artist!" Until she said it, she hadn't been sure.

He froze. Then he stood and faced her. "If he's an artist, what did he paint?"

She tried to hide her fluster. "I don't have to—"

"No, Lily, this time you don't get to walk. We'll settle it once and for all. This is an art museum, right?" He gestured grandly and she yearned to smack the smug look off his face. "If the killer's an artist, something inspired him. Show me a painting sick enough to inspire a maniac to flay and bisect George Kurtz."

She squared off. "The museum's about to close."

"It reopens in the morning."

"What about your flight?"

"There's another one tomorrow."

Chapter Nine

When the museum opened, they met in the lobby. Paul had evidently slept well; he was in a better mood, even jovial. She still smarted. How dare he pity and mock her!

"Where shall we start?" she said.

"With the gore."

"This is a museum, Paul, not an abattoir."

"You're the one who thinks he's an artist." His grin was strained. Was he bristling at being accused of breaking into her condo, or still furious over what happened ten years ago? "Does your museum have a version of *St. Sebastian with the Arrows*?"

"No, but we have more than one crucifixion."

"Let's start there," he said. "You can play your dad's game."

The sooner this charade was over, the better. "You're the one who thinks perfection's bullshit."

"Now's your chance to convince me."

At the Spanish Colonial gallery they wasted no time on the silver or decorative arts. He stopped in front of a twelfth century altarpiece and waited with his arms folded.

"Does it remind you of Kurtz?" he said.

"Not in the least." She turned to leave.

"Not so fast." He was like a kid with a front-row seat to the circus, only to discover there were no clowns. "Think about the body."

Humor him. She looked at Christ on the cross again.

"Kurtz wasn't spread-eagled. When's your flight?"

"Come on, Lily," he chided, "you were trained better than that."

"The display's all wrong. He's nailed to a cross and Kurtz was propped in a chair."

He shook his head. "Another blind alley. What about the ankles?"

"Christ's are crossed and pinned. Kurtz's were broken."

"And?"

"Breaking Kurtz's ankles cut his feet from view. It made the tableau compact." She was getting testy. "That's why I said it's a painting, Paul, not because of the gore."

He held up his hands in mock defense. "Let's look some more."

They took the elevator to the European & American gallery. He stopped at a sixteenth century portrait of a man whose head was a composite of vegetables and fruit. "What about him?" His nose was a zucchini, his lips were grapes, and a glossy eggplant hung from his ear. The artist was Italian, of course.

"Was Kurtz a vegetarian?" she mused. "There *is* something about turning a man into a bowl of fruit."

"The ultimate still life?"

They moved to a Dutch Golden Age painting commemorating a dead soldier. The breastplate was propped up like an armless and legless Kurtz, and the shiny helmet reminded her of his brilliantined hair. A sword's hilt protruded from a swathe of brocade, its blade poised to plow up the breastplate and cut its wearer in two. Medals spilled from a box next to a silver pocket watch.

"Tempus fugit," Paul said, "the transience of life?"

She shook her head. "The killer wasn't honoring Kurtz. He was punishing him."

"But the sword—"

"Too obvious." This was such a waste of time. "He isn't hung up on the seventeenth century, Paul, his inspiration's more modern—almost impressionistic. And it's not about theme. It's about structure."

"Structure?" Maybe it was being around art, but last night's anger and this morning's condescension were gone. Did he want to believe her despite himself? A tour group filed in, led by Dave. He waved but she ignored him.

"Kurtz's arms were splayed on the armrests of his chair, Paul. They converged with the furrow through his sternum and met in a vanishing point at his head."

"Lily—"

They were at the gallery entrance. As usual, visitors flocked to *Seven*.

She stopped.

"What?" he said.

She waited for a break in the crowd, then moved to *Seven*. It was a classic landscape. Grass and wildflowers in the foreground, the deep plow mark leading to the brooding stand of poplars midground to the right. Rooftops in the distance, opposite the trees. Looming clouds. And the little man with the brimmed hat.

"See him?" she said.

"The man? He's heading right into that storm."

"No," she insisted. "He'll make it home."

"But the clouds—"

She stared at the painting. Something had always seemed a tiny bit off. The clouds were moving across the field from the right. The wind came from the same direction, sweeping the poppies and grass towards the viewer and not away. Caillebotte's man was walking directly into the storm. She leaned in closer. And he wasn't heading for the houses. The bend of his knee propelled him ever so slightly toward the trees.

"That's what you wanted me to see?" Paul said.

She stepped back, jostling a visitor. "Sorry," she murmured, and Paul took her arm to steady her. She refocused. "The geometry, Paul. See how the field, furrow and trees converge?"

His grip on her elbow tightened.

"Look at Caillebotte's palette and technique," she continued softly. "The cross-hatched greens and golds, the wet-on-wet poppies, the deep plow mark. Kurtz's killer scored and flayed him and dabbed his intestines on a green silk wall patterned with gold leaves."

"Lily."

"The furrow up Kurtz's sternum is the plow mark here,

the gobs of intestines are those poppies. The green and yellow wall is the field, and that stand of poplars where the field and sky converge is his head."

———

She tied her running shoes. It had been a hell of a day. For a moment in the gallery, he'd seen it too—she'd felt it in his touch, heard his sharp intake of breath. But back in the lab he laughed it off. *Had me going for a minute, Lily. If our burglar paints, I'll let you know.* He really had changed.

She'd spent the rest of the day trying to lose herself in the Degas and waited for rush hour to end to drive home. It had begun snowing again, a spring blizzard on which the drought-stricken Front Range depended. Now three inches of slush blanketed Cheesman Park's running trail. She locked the balcony door. Jack hated to be wet, and it was too late for him to be out. As she stretched at the wall he came up beside her and arched in a perfect imitation of her pose. She scratched his head.

"Back soon."

She set off down the path, gradually adjusting to the snow. She didn't usually run at night but was too keyed up to sleep. Instead of Kurtz and *Seven*, she kept thinking about what Paul said. Not today, the night before. And not just about her but about her dad.

That guilty old...

She passed tall bushes, scattering a flock of sparrows.

Perfection's bullshit. You live in a world of make-believe.

The packed dirt under the slush gave spring to her step. She got into the rhythm of her feet on the trail. The astringent scent of pine needles sharpened by snow carried her past the colonnaded pavilion into what she did best.

On predawn runs back when she was a lawyer, the problems she'd wrestled with were legal ones. Who, what, why. What was different from what she'd thought? *Details, please.* Surrendering to nature on those runs, she'd practiced looking with all her senses: earth versus pavement as she exited the park, a porch light winking on as a man in a bathrobe looked for his newspaper, the purr of an engine turning over and the smell of exhaust from an early commuter heading downtown to work. Then the Zen of running would kick in, freeing her from having to think. By the time she arrived at her office, the answer to her problem always popped into her head. Tonight she didn't want answers. She wanted to escape.

The harder she tried not to think, the more distracted she was. Crossing Sixth, she slipped on a patch of black ice. Did Paul make his flight? She'd kept meaning to return his hanky but couldn't bring herself to launder it. His clove, Jack's perfumed fur... She focused on the streetlights, watching flakes swirl like birds taking flight. He was lying about the case being over, was too smart to believe it was a burglar on crack. Using the distance between lights to get into a rhythm, she timed her steps to her puffs of breath in the cold night air. Was Kurtz really *Seven*?

Details, please.

Why was the little man heading into the storm? Something about the crime scene...

What's hiding in plain sight?

She was getting cold.

Beep!

She flipped off the pickup truck tailing her. The driver sped past, drenching her sweats in sleet. The asphalt was freezing over and it was time to go home to Jack. Twenty minutes later she was in her hallway, unzipping her hoodie and slipping out of her sneakers. A blast of cold hit her. Her sliding door was wide open.

In wet socks, she padded across the rug to close it. Her south-facing balcony had been warmed all week by the sun. Her pots were mounded with snow, but the cement pavers retained enough heat to turn their accumulation to slush. Not enough, however, to erase the footprints leading from the door to the railing. She followed them and looked down.

A black ribbon lay in the snow.

Shoeless, she dashed out her front door and stabbed the elevator button. The elevator was too slow. She ran down the stairs. Wrenching open the emergency door on the south side of the building, she hurtled to the figure in the snow.

Jack was motionless, face-down in a drift. She stroked his head and gently turned him on his back. His eyes were open but unseeing, the jade dull and pupils slits. The luster was gone from his coat and pricks of ice clung to his fur. His chest didn't move.

She kissed his face and breathed on him, trying to warm him. She stroked his stomach and chest and paws. *Make him move, God, anything at all...* Suddenly he convulsed. Violent shivers wracked his tiny body, each worse than the last. She stripped off her hoodie, scooped him up in it and ran to the Prius. With him in her lap, she sped to the 24-hour Vet ER on Broadway.

Chapter Ten

Dave Byers lived along a stretch of Cherry Creek that was once farmland and apple orchards. Now it was two blocks from a Super Target and surrounded by gas stations, Russian supermarkets, and marijuana dispensaries. But the enclave had retained its rural character; in defiance of the high rises looming over them, Dave's neighbors grew squash and corn in their front yards.

Driving there to pick up her dad a month after Kurtz was murdered, Lily marveled at what a good match the two men were. Dave's wit lightened her dad's mood, and they could grouse about developers and the Rockies's pitcher to their hearts' content. This was her first time there, and the address for what Dave had described as a 1950s ranch-style house was poorly marked. She followed the road past a NO OUTLET sign until it dead-ended at a cement culvert at the entrance to the greenbelt.

Spring runoff had flooded the drain pipes, and on this June afternoon the smell of manure rose from the standing water. To the west, a high fence strung with wire prevented access to Four Mile Historic Park. Fitting for Dave, the last stagecoach stop before Denver on the Cherokee Trail was now a pioneer museum that charged admission.

She turned the Prius around and parked behind a Dodge Ram pickup in front of Dave's house. A thicket of irises and native grass overgrew the path to the front door. There was no bell, so she knocked. When there was no answer, she walked around back.

"Dave?"

From a wooden table he waved. She made her way down the slope to him. He wore a wide-brimmed straw hat and his sleeves were rolled up over his tanned, brawny forearms. Blinking in the sun, he looked like a bear coming out of hibernation. On the deck above them, her dad snoozed with a newspaper in his lap. His bad leg rested on an ottoman.

"What's the latest on those break-ins at your condo?" Dave said.

"Nada."

She'd reported both incidents to the cops. She didn't tell them about the birth control pills or her toothbrush, and since nothing was taken they insisted she'd left the balcony door open herself. She couldn't imagine Paul throwing Jack off the balcony—jealous ex-lover, maybe; cat-killer, no—but she'd changed her locks and was glad he'd returned to D.C. for good. The lab was back to normal and she could give her full attention to the Degas. After a week with Gina, even Amy seemed content to be back in the fold.

"What's this city coming to?" Dave shook his head. "Police department's as incompetent as the mayor's office. At least they got the guy who killed Kurtz."

So much for her theory about Kurtz's killer being an artist. With the arrest of the burglar who'd been terrorizing the Denver Country Club area, Kurtz's murder had moved from the front page to occasional updates and then nothing. Even with a suspected link to a ring with an inside man who worked at an alarm company, crack-crazed burglars apparently weren't good copy.

"And that cat of yours," Dave said, "is he okay?"

"Fine, thanks."

It had been touch and go with Jack. He was lucky to have fallen from such a great height into a snow bank; the distance gave him time to spread-eagle before he landed. Ribs cracked and heart and lungs bruised, he spent three days in intensive care. At home, she cleaned him with Baby Wipes. When he was finally able to groom himself again, they celebrated with canned mackerel.

"I don't know about you, Lily, but if there's one thing I can't stand, it's cruelty to animals."

"Amen to that. How was poker?"

"If it wasn't pennies, I'd be risking my retirement."

Her dad's gallon jar had always been filled to the brim with pennies courtesy of good old Walt. How easily Dave had taken his place! She'd known Walt since she was a girl, but what did she know about Dave? He was retired and a widower, she knew that much.

"Where'd you retire from, Dave?"

"Coors. They offered a package too good to refuse, so I took my pension and ran. My wife and I traveled Europe before buying this place. A year later it was cancer." His voice broke when he mentioned his wife. His bond with her dad was deeper than poker.

A hardbound sketchbook lay on the table. It was opened to a study of grasses.

"You draw?" she asked.

"Sketch." He shrugged. "Took a couple classes at the Art Students League, but apparently I'm not very good."

Farther down the hill was a tin shed. Past it and the chicken wire the greenbelt was thick with bushes, wildflowers, and weeds. The ravine sloped up to a biking trail and sun glinted off the gravel on the path. She looked at his sketch again. "I think you caught something here, Dave."

"You and my legions of admirers."

"Who's your favorite artist?"

"Caillebotte, of course." Batting his eyes like a lovesick cow, he did a perfect imitation of Gina Wheelock. "Brooding alienation, disrupted perspectives, distorted interiors. Take a deep breath. Do I smell... *manure?*'"

"Stop!" She was laughing so hard she felt sick.

"What's so funny?" her dad called from the deck.

"Screw the experts, eh, Lily?" Dave said softly. "I knew there was something about you I liked, and that goes double for your old coot of a dad. Can I take him to Black Hawk?"

It took her a moment to connect. Black Hawk was an old mining town. Luring gamblers with all-you-can-eat prime rib, its casinos now mined another kind of gold.

"You set me up with a ringer," he continued. "Don't I deserve a chance to win back the pennies I lost?"

How long had it been since she'd taken her dad to the

mountains? And he loved prime rib. She felt a rush of gratitude for the bearish old docent. "Join us for dinner tonight, Dave?"

"And miss this light?"

———

"You want to go to Black Hawk?" she asked on their way home.

"With that know-it-all?" her dad said.

"What do you two talk about?" *Surely not art.*

"We don't talk, we play poker. He tried to tell me how to grow roses."

Just roses?

"Dave's nosy," he continued. "He asked about your mother."

Oh? She was number one on the taboo list. "What'd you tell him?"

He snorted. "She was killed by a drunk driver. What more is there to say?"

Everything.

What was he like before she died? Did losing her make him vigilant, did the one time he looked away cost her mom her life? After she died, Lily had scoured the bungalow for traces of her, but all she found was the gold compact where it had fallen behind his dresser. How many times did she click it open as a girl, hoping to catch a glimpse of her mom in the mirror? So often the tiny clasp was almost worn out.

"How's Jack?" he asked.

"Eight lives to go.

"That was some crazy fall."

She pulled into his driveway. "Hungry, Dad?"

He was snoring gently. Dave had done him good.

Chapter Eleven

Sipping plum wine at the preview party for the museum's Samurai Exhibition, Lily scanned the crowd. The ticketed event catered by a Japanese restaurant had drawn a mix of patrons, Asian art lovers, and weapons enthusiasts. Squeezing Nick's arm, she strained to be heard over the drums of a local Taiko band. "Ready to go in?"

He wolfed down his sushi. "Sure."

What a relief to date a guy who wasn't a lawyer! Still smarting from the scenes a month earlier with Paul at the lab, she'd tried to keep her new relationship quiet. Amy suspected something, which meant Dave knew too, but this was the first time she and Nick had appeared at a museum event together. Now he jumped the line to hold the door for a snowy-haired matron on an ebony cane. Ignoring the impatient shuffling behind them, the woman patted Nick's cheek. Lily set down her wine and entered the gallery after them. She scarcely recognized the place.

Knocking down and installing exhibits was like remodeling a house. Paintings needed wall space and objects demanded glass. Both required unimpeded traffic flow, narrative coherence, and visual drama. Because space was at a premium and time meant money, what could take weeks or months was telescoped into days. Crates were inspected and unpacked. Gallery walls were torn down and rebuilt, special lighting installed, art mounted or hung, and 75-word labels created for every object and painting. What little story did each piece of art tell? An exhibition was an enchanted world with its own legends and myths.

This gallery's entrance was guarded by a life-sized Samurai in full armor. His helmet was horned, his shoes were covered in bear fur, and his mailed fist held a fan with a blood red Imperial sun. From behind his iron half-mask, he glared at Lily with murderous rage. Nick had gone ahead and was peering at a display case of swords.

"Your boy likes weapons." Paul stood at her elbow with a wine glass.

"What are you doing here?" Lily said. From the distance Gina waved. Her proprietary, infatuated look was one Lily knew well. She'd seen it enough times on her own face in the mirror after a night with Paul. "I thought Kurtz's murder was solved."

"Denver has other attractions." Gina was cooing at a patron but watching them.

"So I see."

"Green was never your color, Lily." He sipped his wine.

"No food or drinks in the gallery."

"Must you ruin everything?" He set down his glass in a corner, where it wouldn't spill. They moved to a display of armor bearing a chrysanthemum crest. "Your kind of exhibit, Lily, all these shields and spears—" Nick had moved to a seven-foot pole topped with a curved blade. "What do you suppose he's thinking?"

"What all men think when they see a gun or knife."

She detached herself from Paul and went after Nick. To maximize display space, this part of the gallery had been reconfigured into a narrow corridor. Suddenly it opened onto a magnificent centerpiece: three life-sized warhorses in full battle regalia with Samurai soldiers astride. On raised scarlet platforms, necks straining and hoofs raised, the horses were poised to charge.

"Whoa!" Nick said. So uncomplicated—she liked that about him.

The black stallion in the middle reared up on hind legs. It had its own mask with horns, flaming brows, and dragon's teeth. Ferocious as they were, a mount-maker had said the horses were plexiglass and two men could lift them. Paul and Gina were now at a case of arrows. In intense discussion, and she bet it wasn't about art.

"Your ex?" Nick said.

"What makes you think that?"

"I saw you together." He looked at Paul curiously, like an engineer trouble-shooting a problem. At least he wasn't the jealous type.

"Old news," she assured him.

"Does he know about me?"

"Just that you're dangerous," she joked.

Nick narrowed his eyes playfully. "Maybe he knows better than you."

Japanese flutes and plaintive singing had replaced the Taiko drums on an endless loop. Cocktails were over. As guests poured in, the heat had risen. Her head spun. *The plum wine?*

Nick took her hand. "Not like the Impressionists, eh?"

The crowd carried them from the horses around a bend to a case of spiked helmets and leather masks with hair. Not all the armor was behind glass; gallery hosts were positioned to make sure there was no touching, but still ... The exhibition designer had totally redone the space, and she struggled to get her bearings. Was this really the same gallery where the blockbuster Van Gogh exhibit had run? The horses were almost directly behind her on the other side of the wall. Through a space between the partitions, she saw visitors gape at them.

The noise was getting worse and the gallery was claustrophobic. She tried a round of her dad's game. *Where did each Van Gogh hang?* But it was no use. When she came face to face with four life-sized Samurai advancing at eye level from behind a velvet rope, she'd had enough.

"Five minutes," Nick begged. "They're showing a film on swords. The Samurai disemboweled themselves."

Gobs of intestine flashed behind him on the wall, and a whiff of excrement brought bile to her throat. But Kurtz wasn't murdered by a Samurai.

"After he slit his abdomen open with a wakizashi—"

"Wakizashi?" she said.

"—a short sword, his assistant cut his throat. He had a cup of sake first and a favorite last meal."

Did Kurtz's killer offer him sake? But Nick's enthusiasm was so infectious, she smiled.

"I'll wait outside."

Just before the exit was a mask the color of dried blood. Its eyeholes were wide and staring. A leather strap was at the throat.

"Remind you of something?" Paul said.

"Croatia."

They'd gone there for leads on the Schiele case. Facing a long weekend in Zagreb, they'd rented a car and driven to the Adriatic coast. The charming seaside town of Rovinj was packed with tourists. To escape the noise and heat, and drawn by a poster of a painting, they wandered into the local museum. They were the only visitors. A woman with mournful eyes and a hacking cough sold them tickets to a special exhibition and pointed to the stairs up. Instead of paintings, the gallery was devoted to medieval torture instruments.

Iron masks, a rusty guillotine, a spiked throne under which a fire could be lit, a thread of metal hooks to be swallowed and yanked up with the intestines. Nothing was roped or behind glass. Each display had a helpful label in English documenting who, what, when, where, and why. And these weren't replicas, they were the real thing. *How about swabbing that Iron Maiden,* Paul said. He took her hand.

Numbly they went from room to room, followed at a discreet distance by the coughing ticket seller. Was she there to ensure they didn't touch anything? Turning, Lily read a different question in the woman's doleful eyes: *Do you feel them suffer?* At that moment, she knew what art meant: instead of killing things, it brought them to life. She squeezed Paul's hand. *I want to be a conservator,* she'd said. *Of what?* he'd asked. *Paintings like the Schieles in Vienna....*

"He didn't torture him," she told Paul now.

"Who?"

"Kurtz."

He started to reach for her hand, but she stepped back.

"You never let go, do you?" he said.

Gina was bearing down on them, her gobsmacked look replaced by a stony glare. "Oh, there you are!" She linked her arm tightly through Paul's. "Isn't our reservation at eight? Of course, if you'd rather skip dinner..."

"We've been talking about Impressionists." He spoke lightly. "Lily thinks they inspire modern artists."

Gina blinked coquettishly. "Is it a trend?"

I hope not.

"Perhaps a new exhibition..." Gina said.

Paul nodded, but he was a million miles away. In Croatia?

The real questions were why *Seven*, and why Kurtz? Did the killer use Caillebotte's painting as a motif, or did *Seven* inspire him to kill?

Chapter Twelve

Sunlight streaming through Nick's bedroom window woke her. Realizing it was Saturday, she settled back onto the pillows. In the shower, he belted out a lusty tune. She reached to the floor for his shirt and wrapped herself in it. Like Paul, he didn't need deodorant; unlike Paul, he had no natural scent. *Can't have it all.* Remembering last night, she stretched luxuriantly. When the water started running in the sink, she padded downstairs to make coffee.

Nick lived in a sturdy brick house with a two-car garage and a lousy yard. Typical bachelor's digs, it had a kitchen that didn't get much use, shelves crammed with *Atlantics* and *Popular Mechanics*, and a daunting electronic sound system. It seemed too big for one person, but if he'd had a wife or girlfriend there was no sign of her now.

She rummaged through the refrigerator. Beer, Dijon, a brown avocado. The freezer had an opened bag of ground French Roast and freezer-burned English muffins. While the coffee perked, she cleared books from the dining room table. Among them was the catalog from an old Caillebotte exhibition at the Kimbell in Fort Worth.

"We should go to more events with your ex." Nick nuzzled her neck. His auburn hair was wet from the shower and he smelled of soap and shampoo. All he was wearing was jeans.

Forget Paul.

"Something turned you on last night," she said, caressing his back. The angry slashes Jack inflicted when he'd jumped

Nick that first time at her condo were finally scabbing over. *I thought that cat was neutered!* he'd howled. Since then they'd gone to his place. "Can I put on more ointment?"

"He was just protecting you."

She poured coffee into mismatched mugs. "I didn't know you liked Caillebotte."

"Just trying to impress the teacher."

He gave her an affectionate nip before accepting his coffee, and she paged through the catalog. It featured two of Caillebotte's most ambitious works. *On the Pont de l'Europe* was a cityscape in his signature violet-blues. A top-hatted gent and a lady with a parasol stood on a bridge which, according to the catalog, was a place for surreptitious *plein air* assignations. A dog trotted towards them, a hind paw outside the frame. *The Floor-Scrapers* was a sepia-toned oil of bare-chested laborers in an elegant Parisian flat. One man's legs were cut off by the frame. Caillebotte had been savaged for that and the workmen's semi-nudity.

"Don't you hate that all the critics see is sex?" Nick said with a wink.

The catalog also contained several of the *Gennevilliers Plain* series, each with scudding clouds over a verdant plowed field. Unlike *Seven*, none had a man in it. As Nick toasted the English muffins and searched for jam, she wandered to the enclosed porch he used as an office. Above his computer stand was a shelf of cloth-covered notebooks. She took one down. It was stamped FIELD BOOK. The pages were filled with diagrams and notes in pencil and ink.

"An engineer's notebook from the 1940s," Nick said. He spread some jam on a muffin for her. The jar's gingham lid looked French, but it came from World Market. "The Old Masters in my field."

A newer notebook had an orange vinyl cover and sketches by a finer hand. Some were contoured and shaded and accented with bold colored ink. Like *études—plein air* studies artists made as *aides-memoire* for landscapes they painted in a studio later.

"Yours?" she said.

He shrugged diffidently. "Nowadays engineers take notes on PCs." He seemed embarrassed about doing it the old way.

"They're projects I worked on, boundaries and maps. My old man talked me into becoming a surveyor, but I got bored and went to engineering school. I miss working in the field but engineering lets me design. And I love ink and paper."

He'd seemed so out of place as a trainee. He was younger than the other provisionals, almost all of whom were women. The training was rigorous, with weekly graded papers, lectures, and presentations on an object or painting of choice. Miss two sessions and you were out. Now his motivation made sense.

"You're an artist!" She reached for another muffin. It, too, was burnt, but at least he'd tried. "That's why you ask about brush stroke and pigments."

He shrugged again. "I like to know how things work."

She looked out the porch window. A mutt was peeing on Nick's crabgrass. A stout woman gestured at the dog, who ignored her. "Want help pulling those weeds?"

"Too late for that," he said. "I need a combine or a tractor."

"You know how to use them?" Something sexy about guys and heavy equipment.

"Hey, I'm a farm boy."

Like Paul. "That's what's in your garage?"

"Garage?"

"I saw the padlock, and you park at the curb."

He laughed. "Sorry, just a bunch of rusty old tools."

Heedless of the woman next door, he reached for her. She slapped his hands away.

Nick sighed. "Guess I'm buying breakfast."

Chapter Thirteen

The taxi door opened. Out swung a pair of feet in sensible shoes, followed by a stout woman with a red face.

"Welcome back, Candace!" he cried. "How was the symposium?"

Candace fanned herself with a newspaper, then reached for her purse. The cabbie popped open his trunk and hauled out an overstuffed wheeled suitcase.

"It's so much warmer here than in Boston, but I'm glad to be home."

What did she expect? It was the end of June, for God's sake. He directed his watering hose to a particularly unruly clump of grass and let it run. To him, roses were no different from weeds. The cabbie set down the suitcase and waited to be paid.

"I do hope Sargon wasn't too much trouble," she called over her shoulder.

"He never is," he assured her. Who named a dachshund after an Assyrian king? An art historian. Candace thought she was *so* clever. She paid the cabbie and he drove off. The suitcase sat in the street. It was too heavy for her to lift over the curb, but he didn't offer to help. "Did your presentation go well?" Something on Syrian antiquities. She'd gone on at length about it, but he hadn't listened.

"Quite. They asked me to deliver it next spring in London."

"Bravo, Candace!"

"I'm sorry I was away so long." She fumbled in her purse

for her keys. "You're a dear to let me visit Denise."

Candace was a widow. Denise, her lumpy daughter in Providence, was her only family. Besides Sargon, of course. How many extra days had she tacked onto her trip? Three, making it a total of ten. More than enough. "You give me far too much credit, Candace."

"I don't know what I'd do without you...."

The first time he'd cared for Sargon it was two days. As Candace's trust in him grew, her number of trips expanded correspondingly. Now she attended every symposium and conference that invited her. Did she think he had no place else to be, nothing better to do? Experts like her were all alike: manipulators of perception and taste. They wouldn't recognize true genius if it bit them on the ass. Which reminded him of Sargon. "No sacrifice is too great for the cause," he murmured. "The world always needs another art historian."

Candace found her keys. Looping her purse over her wrist, she struggled with her bag. One wheel stuck on the curb. As she tugged at it, her agitation excited him. He let his hose play over the grass. He thought of Lily.

The only person more despicable than an expert was a pretender. He'd put her perfect eye to the test and she'd failed. After he broke into her condo, she blamed it on her ex. It took fifteen minutes to flatten those toothbrush bristles to evoke the grass in a Caillebotte! Was she too unobservant to see the connection, or trying to insult him by ignoring his clue? He couldn't possibly have been more direct. That is, until he threw her cat off the balcony.

"Was it this hot the whole time I was gone?" Candace asked.

"A veritable heatwave. Thank God for air conditioning."

Suitcase free at last, she started up her front path. Wrestling her bag to the door, she fumbled again with her keys. Her hands must be trembling in anticipation of being reunited with her beloved dog.

"Did you put ice in Sargon's water?" she asked.

"Those people are experts. I'm sure they know what they're doing."

Keys in the door, she looked at him over her shoulder.

"What people?"

"At the kennel, of course."

"Kennel?" Confusion swept her doughy face. He turned the hose to another patch. "But Sargon isn't at the kennel."

"No?"

"Didn't you—"

"Didn't I what?"

"Didn't you take care of him?"

People believed what they wanted to believe. "Why no, Candace. You said you'd drop him off on the way to the airport. It *was* an awfully long trip."

Candace's keys slipped from her fingers. She scrabbled to retrieve them. Snatching them up, she stared. Confusion turned to terror and her mute plea gave way to comprehension. Just like George Kurtz. She unlocked her door and recoiled from the stench. He shut off his hose. He waited for the scream.

Poor Candace!

This was better than he'd expected—a particularly successful *étude*. He wound up his hose and went inside. It was awfully hot.

Now what did he want for dinner?

Chapter Fourteen

Palette's four-tops were covered with white linen, its carpet evoked Klee, and its entrées were works of art. For each major exhibition, the museum's restaurant and wine bar offered a prix-fixe tasting menu. Van Gogh was fêted with pork terrine and coq au vin. Christian Dior got onion soup and trout amandine. The Samurai's menu was duck salad and Kobe beef.

When Angela Kurtz had called and suggested lunch, Lily was pleasantly surprised. She traded her bomber jacket and sneakers for a sweater set and strand of cultured pearls—Elena always said they came in handy—and now made her way to the table where Angela waited.

"This must be a terrible time," she began.

Angela actually looked great. Her hair was professionally highlighted with blonde streaks, and instead of the Jackie O shades, she wore contacts that made her eyes intensely blue. Her fitted designer sheath complemented her cerise lipstick and shapely bosom, and the zipper up the front had a fetching gap at the neckline, a bold fashion statement for a woman who was reinventing herself. Even the watch on her formerly pudgy wrist was now an ultra-thin pink-gold with an alligator strap.

"You're the only one who bothered to write," Angela said.

"Surely Michel—"

Angela snorted. "Let's get one thing straight. George Kurtz was a prick."

Elena had said as much, but it was shocking to hear it

from his daughter. They ordered salads off the regular menu, and a bottle of wine magically appeared. "The museum certainly appreciates your father's generosity."

"The only altruistic thing he ever did was die."

Good thing my afternoon's clear.

"But it was wonderful of him to donate that Caillebotte. One thing I'm curious about—"

"See that gal?" Angela pointed at a woman with spiky hair at a table in the corner. Gina, with Amy. "If Michel knew the truth, she'd be out on her ass."

But Lily was looking at Amy. Amy with the porcelain skin and pre-Raphaelite curls, the smoky eye shadow and singular focus! Lily's brilliant young Mellon Foundation assistant was endowed in more ways than one. Did her time with Gina last month turn her head? They were giggling conspiratorially.

"Or maybe not," Angela continued. "She thinks sleeping with George is a mark of distinction, but he had something on her, too."

"Sorry, who?"

Angela rolled her eyes.

At sixteen, Amy had placed first in a prestigious competition sponsored by the National Young Arts Foundation. Her unflinching oil of an elderly woman came to define the beauty and ravages of aging. At eighteen, she was a Presidential Scholar in the Arts. On weekends, Lily saw her painting at an easel at the European & American gallery. Art students trained by copying, but Amy had been out of school for years. Now she and Gina rose to leave.

"...launder money," Angela was saying. As she reached to refill their wine glasses, her neckline gaped. Was the zipper coming undone? The last thing a woman starting to care for herself needed was a sartorial faux pas. Lily tapped her pearls to signal her. "All you need is a phony appraisal."

"Pardon?"

"You want to know why George gave the museum that Caillebotte, right?" Angela said patiently. "Charitable trusts are a scam. The higher the appraisal, the bigger the deduction and the closer you get to donating the magic five percent of your assets to satisfy the IRS. When money doesn't change hands, nobody second-guesses an appraisal."

Museum-world's cardinal rule was never ask what anything costs.

"IRS doesn't care," Angela continued. Two more zipper teeth were unfastening. "You're a hero, the museum throws a gala, and the real money goes wherever you want."

"A slush fund?" Lily tapped her pearls more insistently.

Amy and Gina were coming their way. Lily tugged urgently at her pearls. Angela looked at her quizzically, then gave a start. She looked down and zipped up just in time to avoid a fashion disaster. Her lip trembled and she mouthed *thank you.*

"Angela!" Gina cried. "Why didn't you tell me you'd be downtown? We could have lunched. How brave of you to be out and about."

"Hi, Gina," Lily said. *Is that a hickey on her neck?*

Gina blinked like a semaphore. Her relationship with patrons was sacrosanct. Or was she afraid of what they might be talking about? "What are you doing here?"

"Even conservators eat."

"Aren't you the Mad Greens type?"

Angela's eyes darkened. "I invited Lily," she said evenly. "We're discussing paintings."

"Why don't we do that over dinner?" Gina said. "Michel and I—"

"Not business. Art."

Gina recoiled as if she'd been slapped. Angela was no rich girl with daddy issues and a drinking problem, or a shrinking violet finding her place in the sun. Lily looked at Amy.

Want to play in the big leagues, kid? Watch Angela.

"We were discussing Gustave Caillebotte," Lily said, "the thrill of unveiling *Fields of the Gennevilliers Plain, No. Seven.*"

"A conservator's viewpoint is always enlightening," Gina said.

Lily smiled back. "We just do scut work."

Now Amy looked down at her shoes. What was it like to go from Presidential Scholar to scut work in a lab? She deserved better than that and copying masterpieces on her weekends.

"Want to work on the Degas?" Lily said.

"Me?" Amy squeaked. "I'd love to!"

"You can help me clean it. We'll talk later."

Amy and Gina left.

"She's scared," Angela said.

"Amy?"

"Gina. Of you." Angela poured the last of the wine.

"She's not so bad." She was liking Kurtz's daughter more and more. "We were talking about the Caillebotte."

"Ah, yes—the art of the scam. But George particularly liked *Seven*. He hung it in his bedroom."

"How did he acquire it?"

"Through Morley Sullivan."

"Is he still around?"

"Died last year. Here's to the IRS, the museum, and all the politicians George bought."

They raised their glasses in a toast. In a fight over Kurtz's estate between Angela, his ex-wives, and Gina, Lily knew which horse she'd back.

"Who do you think killed your father?"

"Not a burglar," Angela said, "that's for damn sure. I don't care how many country club estates have been hit, how crappy their alarm systems were, or what the guy they arrested was high on. George was cheap, but not with security. He let his murderer in."

"Why?"

"Because he had something George wanted. And what George wanted, he took."

Lily waited.

"He loved inflicting pain. On me, my brother..." Angela's voice caught. "Don't get me wrong, Lily. I want justice." Her gaze was firm, resolute. "I want the killer caught so I can thank him."

Okay then.

"Anyone specific?"

"There was an ugly fight over a company he bought."

The lawsuit Margo mentioned? Corporate acquisitions were knife fights, but they didn't usually end in murder. Lily caught the waitress's eye for the check, but Angela had already paid. Something said they'd be seeing more of each other.

"Did your father have friends?"

"He belonged to the Cactus Club."

She'd been invited to the century-old private men's club for a senior partner's roast. Seated at a narrow table running the length of the room, they slapped their hands on the wood and cried, *Hear, hear!*

"I mean someone who actually liked him."

Angela thought hard. "Rosie."

Chapter Fifteen

In scarlet caftan, black leggings and boots, a ceramic choker with stones like robin's eggs, and yards and yards of turquoise beads, Elena Brandt drew every eye in the Ship Tavern. The man she was with had dyed black hair, a walrus moustache, and a rumpled seersucker blazer. Among the bankers and businessmen in the crowded downtown pub, the two octogenarians were as exotic as a pair of flamingos ringing the New York Stock Exchange's opening bell. Lily made her way to their table.

The mustachioed man rose.

"Anton Petrosian at your service." He was as wide as he was short, and his trousers didn't match his coat. He looked like an Armenian rug merchant. Bowing, he kissed her hand. "I am a connoisseur of women and art. You may call me Rosie."

Elena winked.

"Do you know how Elena and I met?" he asked.

"Rosie..." Elena warned.

His black eyes gleamed. "The Tropics."

"A cruise?" Lily said.

"Finest burlesque joint in Denver." The Armenian had raw sex appeal, and the way he was looking at Elena was unmistakably carnal. "The stage had a hydraulic lift and the girls wore leopard jumpsuits with one shoulder strap. Every hour they made tropical thunder. That gilded birdcage..." Elena blushed furiously. "You were more beautiful than Tempest Storm."

"Elena in leopard skin and a cage?" Lily said.

"That's enough, Rosie! Lily wants to know about George."

"Elena says you saw his body," he said. "How did he look?"

Lily was saved by the waiter.

"Drinks?" he asked.

"Something befitting George..." Rosie drummed his fingers. His jade ring was carved like a scarab. "Pabst Blue Ribbon, canned."

"Coors is closest, bottled or tap," the waiter said. "In cans we have local porters and ales."

"No, no." Rosie shook his head emphatically. "Brewpub ale is too fancy. When George slummed, he did it big. How he loved those tallboys—they made him look badass. It wasn't a side he showed many people."

"Tall boys?" Lily said. *Was Kurtz gay?*

Rosie looked amused. "Not much of a beer drinker, are you?"

"Tallboys are forty-ounce cans, ma'am," the waiter explained. "We don't carry them."

"Bottled Coors, then," Rosie declared.

The Ship Tavern's nautical motif extended from the captain's wheel over the bar to a menu catering to mariners and landlubbers alike. Lily and Elena ordered Starboard Salads, which had bacon instead of seafood. Rosie chose the Authentic Philly Cheesesteak.

"Was George really carved up?" he asked when the waiter left. "Word gets around."

"Well—" Lily said.

"I heard he was filleted with a boning knife. Was it bloody? Those gorgeous celadon silk walls..."

"Rosie, please," Elena said. "Tell Lily what you know."

"George was perverse. He drank canned beer because his father despised it."

"Why Pabst Blue Ribbon?" Lily said. Nowadays it was a retro hipster beer.

"He liked the name. Grandiose—he fancied himself a gourmet, but he had more money than taste. Whatever you wanted, he took. Poor Jay..."

"Jay?" she said.

"Kurtz's son," Elena explained.

"I tried to mentor the boy, but George cast him off like trash. The truth is—"

"Rosie—" Elena warned.

The food arrived. Lily was grateful for the timeout, but she had to get Rosie away from Elena. "Have you seen Kurtz's art collection?" she asked him.

"Oh, yes." Rosie was suddenly preoccupied with his sandwich.

"How did you and Kurtz meet?"

"Come to my shop and I'll tell all," he promised. "Now let us toast dear George."

They raised their bottles of Coors.

"To revenge," Rosie proclaimed. "Unlike a Philly Cheesesteak, a dish best served cold."

Chapter Sixteen

Verdigris lions guarded a cream-colored building onto which vaguely Asian additions had been tacked, rendering its architectural origins tantalizingly mysterious. The windows held a single brass urn and one porcelain vase. Crossing the threshold of Petrosian's Fine Art and Antiquities, Lily entered a vast room filled to the rafters with art.

Rugs from India, Persia, and the Central Asian steppes were rolled and stacked against the walls. Chinese horses and roof tiles, pear-shaped lutes with silk strings, Mongolian armor laced with rows of iron plates. Any sense of order must have been in Rosie's head, for these treasures appeared to be whatever caught his eye. As she ran her fingers over the brass fittings of a Korean blanket chest, Rosie emerged from the back.

"Lily!" He threw out his arms, and his mustache tickled her cheek. "Welcome to my domain. Have you caught George's murderer?"

"Not yet."

"Now it's my turn. Let me show you—"

A woman had followed him out. She was a foot taller than Rosie, and had chin-length white hair, blue eyes and a sphinxlike gaze. She wore a black dress, high-laced shoes and a long silver chain with keys around her neck.

"Ah, Miss Sjostrom!" he cried. She had to be north of sixty. "Scribe, muse and guide extraordinaire."

"Tea?" Her accent was a flat Midwestern.

"That would be lovely," Lily said.

Sjostrom glided off and Rosie took Lily's arm. "She worked for my father," he whispered. "She has a peculiar affection for Native American artifacts, so I collect some baskets and beads. Don't tell Elena, but without Sjostrom I'd be lost."

He walked her through his collection. Each item was precious, from the humblest pottery bowl to the most elegant Persian rug at 1200 knots a square inch. He could—and did— recite its provenance, from the village where it was made, to the family who produced it, to the materials and tools and vegetable dyes they used, and the precise circumstances under which he or his father or grandfather first saw and acquired it. No Petrosian would dream of cutting up a rug to cover an ottoman or footstool. He unfurled an exquisite rug with an intricate floral pattern.

"Take your time," he said.

Lily scrutinized the rug. One peony petal was a slightly darker shade of rose.

"Why is the thread different?" she said.

"Elena was right!" He beamed. "It's a Persian flaw. The weaver embraced his imperfection by introducing a subtle but deliberate mistake. Native American artists insert the wrong color or size bead to show humility, too. It's called a spirit bead."

The tour ended at his carpet-cleaning operation in a renovated auto body shop out back.

In contrast to the hodgepodge in the showroom, here an antiseptic orderliness prevailed. A man in rubber apron and boots hosed down a Kurdish tribal rug in a shallow cement pool. His colleague combed the fringe of a Tabriz with a metal rake as gently as if he were untangling a baby's hair. Rugs of all descriptions hung from tall metal drying racks, and in the background industrial fans ran.

"What does this remind you of, Lily?"

"A carwash for rugs."

"That's all?" He was disappointed. "I think of it as a morgue."

"Well..." She looked around again. "The cement slab could be an autopsy table."

"The hose?" he said.

"Flushes away blood and human waste."

"Precisely! And the rake..."

"To comb a corpse's hair." Test or not, this was fun. "You could hang cadavers from those racks. As for the ceiling fan—"

"—those bodies do get ripe!" He clapped with delight. "Now tell me how George looked."

"You really want to know?"

"Yes, and before tea. Sjostrom has no stomach."

There was no getting out of this. "Kurtz was sitting in a chair..."

Rosie waited.

"...split up the middle from his pelvis to his chest. The rest was flayed."

"Blood?" he asked.

"Gobs," she confirmed, "smeared with his intestines on the wall."

"In his library, papered in silk? Such a waste!" He seemed more dismayed about the damage to the wallpaper than to Kurtz. "Off the top of your head, Lily: who murdered George?"

"*You* knew him—" she protested.

"Exactly my point. Elena says you see things I can't."

Sjostrom had slipped in behind him and was listening intently.

Lily took a deep breath. "I think the killer's an artist."

"Because?" Rosie said.

"He made Kurtz into a landscape."

"Style?"

"Impressionist. The armchair, the flay marks, those gobs on the silk."

He nodded. "Was it an analytical study, with crisp angles and brushstrokes all very precise, very Cezanne? Or an existential howl of rage, like Edvard Munch?"

"If it was rage," Lily said, "I think he enjoyed it." Sjostrom slid off. Now for the quid pro quo. "You said revenge is best served cold."

"He who waits a thousand years is impatient."

"Come on, Rosie."

"In good time, my dear." He patted her arm affectionately. "Sjostrom gets cross if she's kept waiting, and she likes her tea hot."

The tea was brewed from fresh mint leaves boiled on a hot plate in his office. Sjostrom served it in glasses with just-baked Swedish thumbprints with lingonberry jam.

Reinvigorated, Rosie turned to his scribe.

"The key, Sjostrom." She detached a small shiny key from her chain and handed it to him. "You may leave if you like," he said kindly. "You've heard this story before."

Sjostrom settled back in her chair.

"If a picture tells a thousand words, how captivating a story does an object paint?" Rosie took down the Chinese scroll behind his desk and dialed the combination to his safe. He carefully removed a lacquered box about a foot and a half square. He opened the box with Sjostrom's key and placed its contents on his felt blotter.

Lily's breath caught.

The vase was sixteen inches tall. Glazed in translucent jade, it had a primrose yellow neck and its curves were perforated in a sort of basket weave. The medallions on them were enameled with fat golden carp frolicking in rolling waves. Charming as the carp were, what made the vase so irresistible was what lay inside. Through the perforations in the outer wall a second vase could be seen. That vase was Ming, with blue flowers scrolling down white porcelain. It was almost too perfect.

Hubris, Sjostrom mouthed.

"Qianlong Dynasty, circa 1740," Rosie said crisply. "They call the style 'Yangcai' because the colors came from Europe. She's priceless, of course."

She? Lily longed to touch it but didn't dare ask.

"The Emperor who commissioned her was an ascetic. Each day he rose at 6:00 a.m. He breakfasted alone at 8:00, and had another brief and solitary meal at 2:00 p.m. He read, wrote poetry, and painted. He was slim and elegant and wore a yellow silk robe. He was Manchu, of course." He glanced playfully at Sjostrom. "Unlike the Chinese, he took his tea with milk from a special herd of dairy cows. Thanks to a devoted servant who was apparently a hermaphrodite, he lived to the age of eighty-nine."

Sjostrom snorted.

"Where did you find the vase?" Lily asked.

He wagged his finger. "Did Elena teach you nothing? Let's just say we met on a trip, and I made the mistake of telling George. For reasons as to which I can only speculate, he informed the U.S. Customs Service. They confiscated the vase and charged me with some nonsense over an improper form. It took six years and a fortune in legal fees to get her back. Lord knows what she was subjected to in captivity."

"Pity to lock her away," Lily said.

"She wasn't safe with George alive."

"What will you do with her now?"

He looked at Lily for a long moment. "Donate her to the museum, if the right person asks." Sjostrom nodded briskly before pouring more tea and passing the cookies again.

"Why did Kurtz betray you?" Lily asked.

"George fell in love with the Emperor. He physically resembled him, you know—tall and thin, the same aquiline nose. In private, he started wearing a yellow silk robe. If only he could have found a hermaphrodite!" Rosie seemed more amused than aggrieved. "His attraction to the Emperor was erotic, of course; they both had to possess the objects of their passion through any means necessary. George lusted after the vase because the Emperor owned it. I refused to sell it to him."

"That's it?" Lily said.

"Of course not. Close your ears, Sjostrom."

She and Sjostrom leaned forward.

"George liked The Tropics, too, and he was wild for Elena. Maybe it was that gilded cage." Rosie's eyes glittered like jet beads. "I took her from him, so he took the vase from me. But that's ancient history."

Or so he wanted her to think. At the gala, Kurtz's interest had felt more predatory than erotic. And no matter how hot Elena was back in the day, it was hard to imagine Kurtz making a serious play for her, or her giving him more than a glance. A man who wore yellow silk and fantasized about hermaphrodites might have shocked even Elena.

"What happened to Kurtz's son?" Lily asked. "Wasn't he

pleasing enough?"

Rosie's laugh was unexpectedly harsh. "Jay was as beautiful as this vase."

"Then why—"

"He hated Jay because he envied him."

"Why envy his own son?"

"Because Jay had nothing to lose."

Sjostrom poured the last of the tea.

"Who do you think killed Kurtz?" Lily said.

Rosie twirled his moustache. "An artist he insulted, the living portrait of *The Scream.*"

Sjostrom burst into laughter.

"What's so funny?" he said.

"You two are missing the point!" Sjostrom said. "The art world's filled with wounded souls like Munch's."

Rosie's whiskers twitched. "Then who is he?"

"An art forger."

"Ah, Sjostrom." He patted his stomach and sighed like Escoffier contemplating a fine pâté.

"Talk about soul murder," Sjostrom insisted. "A forger doesn't do it for money. He does it to prove a point. The art world rejected him and he must prove the experts wrong."

"What makes you so sure it's a man?" Lily asked.

"Forgers usually are." Sjostrom smiled regally. "And he and Kurtz are two of a kind."

"Meaning?"

"Hubris."

"But we're talking murder!" Rosie cried.

"Precisely."

Chapter Seventeen

Undulating shoulder to knee, Paul surged across the pool. Two breaths carried him to the wall, where he executed a perfect flip and continued without missing a beat. She'd forgotten butterfly was his stroke, that he'd been captain of his college team. As he ricocheted from one end of the pool to the other, it was like watching an Olympic ping-pong player compete against himself.

She'd called him after leaving Rosie's, and he suggested meeting in the Ritz-Carlton lobby at five p.m. Arriving early, she was directed to the athletic club next door. In the lull between late-lunchers and the after-work crowd, he clearly hadn't expected an audience. As he climbed from the pool in his knee-length Lycra swim shorts and stripped off his goggles, he quickly hid his surprise. "Care to join me?" He spoke easily but his shoulders heaved. "Salt's good for the skin."

"Another time."

He reached for his towel, then paused. His skin was ruddy and water beaded the wiry curls on his chest. The salt enhanced his scent, added a tang to his sweat. Fresh from his goggles, his eyes were dilated. They stared at her now. He was never sexier than after a workout; exercise burned off that professional edge, gave vent to his athleticism and frustrations. And in his Lycra shorts...

He pulled off his swim cap and brushed his hair from his forehead. As he adjusted to the bright overhead light, he blinked. In three seconds he'd be the man who was sleeping with Gina.

"Join me in the hot tub," he said. *One.* "This time of day, you don't need a suit." *Two.* "Or we can book a couples massage at the hotel spa." *Three.* "Afterwards—"

She picked up his towel and flung it at his midsection. "You'll catch cold, if you haven't already."

It took willpower for him not to glance down. "Can I shower?"

"This won't take long."

He tied the towel around his waist and sat on the bench.

"I spoke with an old friend of Kurtz's." She recounted her meeting with Rosie.

"You think the killer's a rug salesman?"

"Of course not!" She couldn't imagine Rosie wielding anything more lethal than a bamboo pen. "But Kurtz had enemies."

"I'll check into whether Denver has enough Armenians to make a mob." He rubbed the stubble on his chin and started to rise. His workout flush was gone, and he had gooseflesh— this time for real. In five minutes he'd be in his room shaving for dinner. A date with Gina?

"I have another lead, Paul."

"Kurtz's son?" He shook his head. "Jay's been dead for five years."

"Maybe it was someone he knew."

He smiled condescendingly. The balance of power had shifted the moment he donned that damned towel. Now he stood, not in the least self-conscious about the state of his balls. "Sure you don't want a massage? Hotel spa has a Mile High Malt Scrub with a beer mask, and you love a good microbrew...."

"You know I hate beer." But it reminded her of something. "Kurtz had a weakness, Paul. It's sold at ballfields."

He wiggled his eyebrows. "Hotdogs and peanuts?"

"Canned beer. Pabst Blue Ribbon."

"Lily, for Christ's sake—"

"I'm serious. Rosie knew him well."

He sat again. "Okay. What's your real lead?"

"What if the killer's an art forger?"

"Forgers aren't violent, Lily." She hated that patronizing

tone. "Their victims are institutions and rich people who want to be deceived. Every collector dreams of finding a masterpiece. When he does, he wants it to be real."

But Paul was right: the art world's hubris ensured only the clumsiest forgeries were caught. An art historian or dealer could analyze stroke, pigment, and themes till the cows came home, but as often as not authentication depended on a "feeling". Rival experts could be played off against each other. Tell one his competitor thought a painting was fake, and he'd say it was real. Even if you subjected the canvas to forensic tests, a forger could defeat them by using period materials.

"...Robin Hood. Catch one and he becomes a folk hero," Paul was saying. "What's gotten into you, Lily? First you think Caillebotte inspired Kurtz's killer, now he's a forger." He winked. "Tell you what. If the Armenian mob pans out, I'll take you to the swankest steakhouse in town..."

"You already did, and I didn't get to order."

"...and if it doesn't pan out, you'll give me something I want."

"A dozen cigars?"

He smiled indulgently. "You'll stop seeing Nick Lang."

"What?"

"He's not right for you, Lily. I don't want you to get hurt."

"You prick!"

A guy in a Speedo and a girl in a tank suit were coming out of the locker rooms.

"Want to know why?" he continued. The swimmers dangled their feet in the pool, pretending not to listen.

"Go back to D.C.!"

"You really want that, Lily?" He was playing to them. "How about dinner instead?"

"How about doing your job?"

His eyes flashed. "My job?"

"That burglar's bullshit and you know it. Are you throwing this case?"

———

Paul looked at his watch. Nine o'clock Denver time, which meant 11:00 p.m. in D.C. The person he reported to kept late hours. He took his drink to a booth and hit the speed dial.

"Senator Grace," he said.

"Paul! How nice of you to call."

He did that every night when he had something to report. In her background were voices and tinkling glass. He wasn't about to tell her Lily's crazy idea, but he had to give her something. "I'm running down a lead, Senator."

"I wish you'd call me Susan. How many times must I ask?"

She wasn't technically his superior, but as the ranking minority member of the Senate Committee on the Judiciary and the subcommittee on Crime and Terrorism, she might as well be. He simply could not call her Susan, nor was he accustomed to reporting to anyone but the FBI's chain of command. But she'd been steering plum assignments his way for years and asked nothing in return. Until now.

"Still working with the locals?" she said.

They'd been over this before. How could a former prosecutor not understand that cutting the locals out of the loop was impossible—and stupid? "They've been helpful."

"You're my eyes and ears on the ground." She was in a huff. "If I wanted to rely on the Denver cops, you wouldn't be assigned to this case!" She sighed. "Wrap this up, Paul. You're more valuable here."

Was she referring to his testimony eight years earlier on campaign finance law enforcement? It was basically a recap of the tax code, but he'd labored over it. Later she'd summoned him to her office. *You handled that beautifully,* she said, *with such sincerity. Want to go places, Paul?* She searched his face. For what? The senator smiled, and then he knew. *She smells the barnyard on me. I am a dead man walking....*

"Enjoying Denver, Paul?" she asked now.

Like a root canal. "Interesting town."

"I'm sure it's changed in ten years. Weren't you there on a case?"

Did she know about Lily? His divorce had never come up on a review. "The traffic's worse. Now, about that lead—"

"Are you happy, Paul?" The background noise had stopped. She'd moved to another room.

"Beg pardon?" he said.

"I told them to put you up at the Ritz."

"Generous of you, Senator." The suite was the size of his D.C. apartment. He felt kept.

"George Kurtz has important friends."

Has?

"I assure you his investigation is getting the utmost—"

"This case can make or break a career, Paul."

"I appreciate that, Senator," he said crisply. "The new lead relates to Kurtz's son. Before the boy died, he apparently walked on the wild side."

"Excellent! He and the burglar make two good prospects."

Prospects? His 25-year-old bourbon suddenly tasted like Jim Beam.

"Good night, Susan."

Chapter Eighteen

Lily dipped her swab in solvent and rolled it in a tiny circle over the edge of the ballerina's tutu. She made her own swabs from cotton wool wound onto a thin wooden stick. After each pass, she inspected the bud to make sure she was removing nicotine and varnish, and not paint. Varnish was impossible to remove completely, and Degas's chalky oils had made the surface thirsty. The ballerina's varnish had sunk into the paint.

To prevent contaminating the canvas with residue, she disposed of the cotton in a container with a lid. Then she wrapped a fresh bud around the stick and repeated the process. She should have worn gloves to protect her hands, but cotton was slippery and gloves made it easy to underestimate her grip and force. At night she repaired her hands with an emollient cream.

She gave Amy the loupe.

"May I?" Amy said.

"Of course."

She watched Amy inspect the Degas. Since that day at Palette's, Amy had been helping her clean it. The loupe hovered over the toe shoes.

"The satin gleams..." Amy said.

"...but dully, as Degas intended."

Because each pigment responded differently to the solvent, she'd divided the painting into sections: the ballerina's hair—now a soft auburn, instead of an indeterminate brown—her satin slippers, the wall behind the barre. The job was complicated by filaments of cotton wool embedded in the varnish and the fingerprints of whomever had applied it. But inches at a time, the little dancer had slowly awakened.

The fume extractor over the heat vacuum table abruptly came on. The duct was bigger than an elephant's trunk and the system ran for minutes at a time, muffling all sound. Other conservators wore headphones to drown out the noise; she liked to keep an ear on her surroundings. Now the elephant's roar seemed to trumpet her own thrill and pride in bringing the ballerina to life. As she'd suspected, the tutu's pink was shot with gold.

"Wow!" Amy said. "How did he do that?"

An aura suffused the delicate pink. Unvarnished, the painting's surface was tender, velvety. Like the little dancer herself. Amy's fingers twitched.

"Want to help me revarnish her?" Lily said.

"Oh my God—can I?"

Revarnishing the Degas was the final step. Much as Lily hated doing it, her mandate was clear: The trustee who owned the painting had been unequivocal and Michel had backed him up. But the little ballerina was just beginning to breathe. She deserved the lightest touch.

I am a conservator, not a restorer.

To suit a collector's taste, restorers thought nothing of painting fig leaves over genitalia in an Old Master. Unscrupulous ones even altered stolen works to reintroduce them into the market. But conservators were of a different stripe. They honored the artist's intent, not a collector's whim. Their every act had to be reversible. Each step, including the materials and equipment used, was documented with notes and photographs. No conservator in her right mind would want to replace the tar and yellowed varnish she'd so painstakingly removed, but training and discipline prevailed.

"Which varnish would you use?" she asked Amy.

"Matte."

"Why?" she said.

"That's what Degas would do, if he used varnish at all. Which he didn't."

"Because?"

"Gloss detracts from a painting," Amy recited. "It heightens colors and makes them brighter than the artist intended."

"We'll start with a tiny spot. By hand. Not the spray bath."

"Of course."

With a painting like the Degas, spot-varnishing with a brush was the only way to proceed. The spray bath applied varnish in a uniform stream under a vacuum hood, and the saturated surface it created would destroy the nuances of Degas's delicate strokes. To ensure the proper varnish was applied, each type was loaded into the bath under its own code. Even with that safeguard, Lily always double-checked it.

"And she needs time to cure," she reminded Amy. "The drier the surface—"

"—the less varnish it absorbs and the more matte the result."

Lily switched off the lamps and went to her office. Amy's imminent departure from the nest exacerbated her own postpartum funk, and Paul's blowing off her leads still rankled. She shuffled through papers on her desk, then scanned her e-mails.

2:30 p.m. She scrolled through the crime scene photos, pausing at a close-up of the chair against the wall. That furrow up Kurtz's torso, his splayed arms converging at his brilliantined poplar-head...

2:42. She called Nick.

Nick Lang. Leave a message.

"It's me," she said brightly. "Can I bring a takeout?" Feeling foolish, she hung up.

She logged onto the museum's database to see if it had anything on the ballerina. It was in the trustee's private collection, at least until Michel pried it from his cold, dead, nicotine-stained fingers. What idiot had coated it with that godawful varnish? Nothing.

2:56. Too early to go home.

She hopscotched through the European & American collection. At *Seven,* she paused. It was presumed to have been painted in 1884, after Caillebotte retired to Petit-Gennevilliers and did the six other landscapes in the series; that it was undated and unsigned wasn't unusual for him or his contemporaries. Was it just a pawn in Kurtz's tax-evasion scheme, as Angela said? But something drew him to that canvas and put them both in the murderer's path. Every painting had a story. The art world called it provenance.

Constructing and deconstructing provenance was itself an art, and the Schiele had given her a taste of the detective work required. Working with Paul taught her one thing: faking a provenance was harder than forging a painting itself, because you had to rewrite history by salting the record with things you made up. Even assembling a legitimate provenance required skill, patience and luck.

Dates, places, buyers and sellers were historical facts that could be ferreted from libraries, databases and catalogues raisonnés. Like stamps on a passport or stickers on a steamer trunk, labels on the back of a canvas or frame were a visual record of when and where a painting was exhibited. Because the art world thrived on secrecy, labels were often coded. Compounding the challenge, an unbroken chain of ownership was the exception and not the rule. What was *Seven*'s story? She dove into the museum's annotated database.

Elena always said the more provenance, the better; assuring a buyer a work was authentic and providing a sexy history increased its value and cachet. *Seven*'s notes did not disappoint. Lily read through its provenance twice. Starting with Caillebotte and working her way up to Kurtz, then from Kurtz backwards on down.

Caillebotte had no direct descendent. When he died of a stroke at age forty-five in 1894, *Seven* went to a woman named Charlotte Berthier. Charlotte left *Seven* to a nephew who died in 1918 on the Western Front. In 1929, the nephew's stepsister sold it to a collector in Paris whose family held it for the next eighty years. Because the collector's grandson couldn't afford to insure the painting, he sold it to Kurtz. Until then, *Seven* had never been publicly shown. Because it wasn't listed in Caillebotte's catalogue raisonné, Morley Sullivan demanded proof that it was authentic.

The collector's grandson produced two expert opinions and an affidavit his grandfather wrote in 1936. Granddad had seen a handwritten letter from Caillebotte to Monet dated July 1884, in which Caillebotte described *Seven* as a breakthrough and the last in his *Gennevilliers Plain* series. Finally, Caillebotte's sketchbook was said to contain an early study of *Seven*.

What's missing that should be there?

Seven's provenance was a handful of data points: 1884, Monet, Charlotte Berthier, a Parisian collector in 1929, his affidavit in 1936, the sketchbook. Why didn't the collector show the painting, or lend it to a museum?

"What are you doing?" Amy was at the door.

"Reading up on *Seven*."

"Why?"

"There's more to a painting than pigment and brush stroke, Amy."

"I know that, Lily! I thought you respected my work."

"Of course I do. That's not—"

"Dave understands!"

Is she having guy trouble? "I'm letting you work on the Degas."

Amy looked down. "Need anything before I go?"

"No, have a great weekend."

"I'll lock up."

Despite the gaps, *Seven* seemed pretty straightforward. *But what about Caillebotte, the man?*

In photos, he was small and round-shouldered. He had a pointed face and chin, ears flush to his skull, and a gaze like a fox. His affluent father built him a studio with a balcony and skylight. At age twenty-five, he was accepted at the Academy des Beaux Arts. But instead of according him the recognition given Monet, Renoir and Degas, critics savaged him.

Early recognition was a curse—look at Amy, copying masterpieces years after winning her big prize. Did it crush Caillebotte?

In 1881, he retreated to a timber-and-stone house with a red tile roof at Petit-Gennevilliers. During his "lost years" of the mid-1880s, he produced his only known sketchbook, painted the *Gennevilliers Plain* series, and in June 1883 wrote to Monet about his struggles with landscapes. A letter survived: *For the two months that I have been here I have worked as much as I could—but everything I do is really bad.*

How bad could a genius's work be?

The Art Institute of Chicago had posted Caillebotte's sketchbook on the web. Forty drawings in graphite and watercolor: panoramas and forests, a village and church, pollarded willow trees. None of the studies resembled *Seven* or contained a man. Two works stood out: a sensitive portrait of a prepubescent boy, and a woman at an open window. The boy's face was softly shaded. His lips were tender. He had a rounded chin and wore a floppy bow at the collar of what could have been a choir robe. The woman was far less detailed; the balustrade on which she leaned was more distinct than she was.

Why didn't he marry?

She searched for Charlotte Berthier and up popped two paintings: Renoir's *Mademoiselle Charlotte Berthier* and Caillebotte's *Madame Anne-Marie Hagen.*

Renoir's *Charlotte* was as frothy and French as her name. Round-faced, rosy-cheeked and plump like all of Renoir's women, she posed in the summer of 1883 in a plumed bonnet and pink frock with a small dog in her lap. Doe-like eyes gazing down and to the side made her seem timid, a trifle out of her element. Caillebotte's *Madame Hagen*, on the other hand, was anything but. Her very name echoed the directness of her stare and the Teutonic severity of her high-necked navy silk dress and black velvet hat. All she needed was a riding crop or whip. Could they be the same woman?

A few more clicks produced the answer. When Caillebotte left Charlotte an annuity and his house in Petit-Gennevilliers, his brothers affirmed in a notarized document that she and Anne-Marie were one woman whose real name was Hagen. Did he reinvent severe Anne-Marie as saccharine Charlotte to maintain his bourgeois respectability in Petit-Gennevilliers? Was mannish Madame Hagan more to his taste?

Lily leaned back in her chair. Kurtz wasn't the only one with a kinky private life, but at least the circumstances surrounding his acquisition of *Seven* rang true. Insuring

Impressionist masterpieces was astronomically expensive. Kurtz did buy exclusively through Sully, an Impressionist expert, and Elena said Sully was no fool....

But what drew Kurtz to Seven?

Kurtz was always in search of a conquest. He'd coveted the Qianlong vase because he fell for the Manchu Emperor. Did the mystery surrounding Charlotte lure him, or was he attracted to Caillebotte himself?

And Sjostrom's theory?

Caillebotte was a forger's dream. He was wealthy enough to be under no pressure to sell, and his small body of work was scattered. But why choose him specifically? *Forgers don't do it for money, they do it to prove a point.* Lily itched to take *Seven* down and properly examine it. The gallery was closed, but Monday—

"Hey."

She looked up.

"Got tired of waiting for takeout," Nick said. "I saw Amy downstairs. She let me in."

Lily grabbed her backpack and they walked out. At the heat vacuum table, Nick stopped. There lay the ballerina on her coverlet.

"I could get into that." His leer was almost as convincing as Paul's. "Pity to varnish her."

The dancer losing her innocence all over again reminded her of Jack. He'd physically recovered from his fall, but his assailant had robbed him of his swagger.

She shivered.

"Cold?" Nick put his arm around her. He was looking at the double-wide table's dual controls. "A king-sized sleep number bed with a quilt! How about trying it out?" His grip tightened, and he nipped her hard on the neck. She drew back. His blue eyes seemed darker, almost black. He was staring at the ballerina. "I bet she'd like to watch."

"*What?*"

Just as suddenly, he was Nick again. He flashed his roguish grin. "Guess I need to work on my lines."

With a last look at the ballerina, Lily switched off the light and locked the door behind them.

Chapter Nineteen

First came the line.

As he drew his pencil slowly across the paper, he reminded himself of two truths: Every great painting begins with a drawing, and every drawing begins with a line. What did the line depend on? A wise professor said comprehension came with proficiency.

Practice, practice, practice.

No artist achieved spontaneity without practice, not even Caillebotte. He sketched in graphite, charcoal and oil. He based his landscapes on *plein air études* and finished them in his studio later. He obsessively relocated his borders, vertically bisecting one boulevardier striding self-importantly out of the frame and reducing another to a pair of legs under an umbrella. His compositions were grand experiments, all part of the fun.

He squinted at the vase he was sketching. He elongated the line, then shaded it with the side of his pencil. The curve still wasn't right. The line should be thinner, of equidistant width. He went back to using the tip. Compositional alterations had a lovely name: *pentimenti,* the artist's regrets. Working on a head or a hand, an Old Master might rapidly sketch different positions and superimpose them over each other on his paper or canvas as he finessed the line. *Pentimenti* could lurk for centuries, reemerging when the paint became transparent with age; as windows into the Master's creative process and intent, they made a painting real. And they endured as relics of his refinement of vision, his smoothing and sharpening of the image, just as a forger honed his blade. He laughed at his bon mot.

Forger—honorable in one trade, despicable in another. So unfair, such a myth! He bore down too hard with his pencil. The tip broke and gouged the cream paper. He started again on a fresh part of the page.

A forger isn't an artist.

To fool the experts, you had to be twice as skilled as the Master himself. First you ruthlessly analyzed your own style to eliminate your mannerisms and "signature." Next came tempo: replicating the ease and speed of the Master's stroke. You picked a painting and copied it as quickly as possible, or deconstructed the artist's process and—*practice, practice, practice*—followed his path. Flow was crucial; without it, the lines were heavy-handed and stiff. A fluid, sinuous line in one part of the canvas and an awkward, hesitant one elsewhere was how you got caught.

A forger lacks passion.

They'd have you believe a successful forgery was a bag of tricks! But once you mastered style, the final canvas couldn't just be a copy. Like *Seven*, it had to be better than the other six. A convincing provenance required more research. In Chicago they'd made him wear gloves to look at Caillebotte's sketchbook. Four sheets in front of the choirboy had been torn out, but the stubs still showed traces of graphite. *What didn't he want the world to see?* No sketches, of course, of the male nudes toweling themselves after a bath that he'd painted at the same time. Nor any trace of so-called Charlotte Berthier, the dominatrix he'd reinvented as his beard! No, when he'd read Caillebotte's June 1883 letter to Monet bitching about his landscapes, he immediately knew what was missing.

Caillebotte needed a man to make it real.

It had been child's play to fabricate a second letter to Monet dated a year later, in which Caillebotte tantalizingly mentioned a breakthrough. He'd painted the mysterious little man hurrying to the trees in *Seven* to entice Kurtz, adding a brimmed hat worthy of Caillebotte himself. How Caillebotte loved his hats! Top hats, sailing caps, straw boaters…. How could Kurtz resist? Why, *Seven*'s little man was as seductive as Junie, whom he'd used to lure his own father! The memory made him frown again.

Creativity was so easily destroyed, the call so fleeting and ephemeral. He had a soft spot for young artists, especially those who feared their best work was behind them. But there was more than one way to get inspiration back. He himself had never felt so productive or fulfilled as now. So fertile... His frown deepened.

Width created volume. To capture the vase's contour, he turned the pencil on its side and shaded with the edge. But the broken tip had left a ridge. When he tried to soften the line, it smudged and the graphite on his hand soiled the paper. Soiled—like Jay Kurtz, whom he'd known from the bars. Jay had told him about his father's hypocrisy and pretentions, the yellow silk robe he wore in private. When he met Kurtz at the Kimbell in Fort Worth later, after Jay had died, it was as if he already knew him. Like a line, an idea had begun to form.

He started on the vase again.

Speeded up, his stroke was less halting and more assured. Closer to Caillebotte's—but just as suddenly, the Master fled. *Who am I kidding?* He tore out the page and crumpled it up. He tossed the soiled effort in the trash. He knew exactly how Caillebotte felt. And Jay.

He gathered his pencils and sketchbook. Opening the door, he braced for a dog's bark. But there was silence. It was weeks since he'd seen Candace. Once when he was in his yard she'd poked her head out the door. Seeing him, she scuttled back in. A few days later a cab came and she left with suitcases. How long before the *For Sale* sign went up? He hoped his new neighbors had kids.

Au revoir, Candace. She'd been good for limbering up, honing his blade. An *étude.* Now he had a more interesting work in progress. Not like his old man, nor his annoying but ultimately harmless neighbor, nor Kurtz who'd needed a lesson. Too bad Jay wasn't around to see it! Kurtz in particular had expanded his portfolio.

But Lily was different.

She'd ignored his labors with her toothbrush. For that insult her cat paid the price. She'd refused to let well enough alone. Looking into Kurtz was dangerous, but her choice again. What came next would be her own fault. He glanced up at the sky. Clouds were moving in. Best pack up for the day.

If *pentimenti* were regrets, for her he had none.

Chapter Twenty

"Don't burglars get lawyers in Denver?" Paul said.

Johnson, the lead detective, shrugged. "Public defender."

They were in Johnson's office at Denver Police headquarters. Paul hid his impatience; the FBI had no jurisdiction over Kurtz's murder, and he understood why the locals wanted to pin it on a guy caught red-handed by a gun-toting country club homeowner. But the crimes had nothing in common, and no forensics tied the burglar to Kurtz. The only leads were the trace chemicals in Kurtz's wounds and the methane used to gas him.

"The library's next to the garage," Paul said. "You ruled out fuel vapors?"

"Kurtz's garage has its own HVAC."

The crime scene was above the cellar, where heavy gases collected, and he bet it wasn't as fancy as the garage. "You checked drains and pipes? Any cracks in plumbing lines or vents?"

Johnson scribbled on a pad.

"What about septic tanks?" Paul said.

Johnson jotted another note, and Paul wanted to throttle his fat throat. The DPD would be better off hiring a plumber. But it was unlikely Kurtz was accidently gassed. Sewer gas contained hydrogen sulfide, which smelled like rotten eggs. And why use methane, or gas Kurtz at all? There were easier ways to disable an eighty-year-old.

"We tested the air in the house," Johnson said. "It was stuffy, but so was Kurtz." He grinned, and Paul gritted his teeth.

He hated everything about this case. How dare Lily accuse him of throwing it? The Senator made it an FBI priority, but he couldn't care less if Kurtz had been slipping her money or anything else. He'd agreed to go to Denver, though for the life of him he couldn't understand why.

Johnson offered him a donut. "Woman trouble?"

I should have told her I was married.

After Lily kicked him out, he'd gone back to D.C. and confessed to his wife. With no kids the divorce was quick and painless. Since then he'd put everything into his career. *Focus.* "Methane comes from compost, waste pits, water treatment plants, horse manure. You can inhale or ingest it."

"I dunno," Johnson said. "Can you picture Kurtz eating rotten bananas, dirt or shit?"

"You have a point." The donut wasn't bad either. Johnson slid the carton over.

The first couple years, he'd called her over and over. She never returned his messages and finally he'd moved on. Granted, to a series of one-week stands, but he had neither the time nor desire for anything real. Not like they'd had. The Schiele nude flashed in his head but he blinked it away. "What about those trace chemicals?" He'd sent samples to the FBI lab.

"Formaldehyde's pretty common."

So now Johnson was a chemist. "It wasn't just formaldehyde. Did you find anything with all three chemicals? And how did they get in Kurtz's wounds?"

Johnson set down his mug and rocked back in his chair. "You seriously expect me to inventory and test every product in his house?"

Yes.

Paul ached to call in his own team. He was juggling cases in D.C., but Susan Grace had made her priorities clear. But Kurtz wasn't butchered and flayed by a burglar. Having gotten away with it once, the killer could do it again. And there was Lily... The Schiele came back more insistently, refusing to be blinked away. Witnessing Lily awaken to her own power that night in the conference room was more erotic than any watercolor nude. In front of that damn Caillebotte with her the other day, he'd felt it again.... *Get a fucking grip.* "Where are we on Nick Lang?"

"He's been under surveillance for weeks."

"Around the clock?"

Johnson looked at him with something like pity. "Enough to know that expert of yours is spending quite a bit of time at his place."

"My expert?"

"That cute little blonde you brought to the crime scene. You didn't mention she works at the museum."

Paul felt himself flush. What was he—sixteen years old? He'd blown every conceivable chance with her, but what hurt most was she evidently believed he was sleeping with Gina Wheelock. *She thinks so little of me.*

"Ms. Sparks is an FBI resource."

"Whatever." Johnson sighed. "We don't have your manpower, son, and it's damn hard to allocate it to a wild goose chase. Particularly one involving—"

Paul rubbed his neck. "I'm not sleeping with her."

"I can see that. But she's affecting your judgment."

"Nick Lang has a motive," he insisted.

"Because he was suing Kurtz?"

"I need to get inside—"

"If you want to search his place, we need a warrant."

Johnson was right. The Schiele faded, and Paul reached for the blow-ups on the desk. Something nagged. Not the glossies of a skinless Kurtz in that chair, or the disgusting gobs on the wall... He stopped at a shot of the divan in the library. He remembered that coat and fedora on it. Kurtz's maid said they were Kurtz's. Why weren't they hanging in his closet?

"Did he take walks before bed?" Paul asked. "Maybe someone followed him home."

"No forced entry."

"Maybe it was a pick-up...."

"... who happened to be carrying a tank of methane gas? Chrissake, Paul, the guy had three exes!"

Paul sighed. "We need to look into Jay Kurtz's friends."

"Why?"

So I can take a woman who despises me to the swankest

steakhouse in town.

"The kid drank himself to death," Paul said. "Maybe a friend bore a grudge."

Johnson snorted. "Gutting a man and smearing his shit on a wall is a helluva payback for a grudge. This wouldn't be another of your girlfriend's—"

"Of course not!" If he told Johnson about the Armenian rug dealer he'd never hear the end of it. "But if Jay had a pal who blamed Kurtz for his death, prudence dictates eliminating him."

"Prudence?" Johnson's eyes gleamed. "So that's her name."

"Just check the bars, for Christ's sake. Drinks are on me."

———

Paul looked at his cell phone. Two messages from Susan Grace.

"Senator?" he said. Another party in the background. Campaigns began on election day.

"Did you look into George's son?" she said.

George. Paul described the efforts to locate Jay Kurtz's friends.

"But you have that burglar."

"The killer wasn't a burglar," he said patiently. "He had finesse."

"Finesse?"

"Artistry." He winced. Now he was thinking like Lily, the last person he wanted on Susan Grace's radar screen.

"Wrap this up, Paul." Laughter rang through the phone. Which K Street gun was footing the bill? "I don't care who it is. A bird in the hand is worth two in the bag—and you have two birds."

What will she do when neither comes home to roost?

"I'm looking at someone else," he said.

"Who?"

"An engineer named Nick Lang."

"Why?"

"He was suing Kurtz and it got ugly." The missing pieces were why Kurtz let Lang in, and how he gassed him. But she didn't need to know that.

"George would've swatted him like a fly, Paul. Don't worry about charges. I'll come up with something to hold him."

"Hold whom?"

"The burglar. I have informants."

Is she kidding—or setting me up?

"Burglary isn't a federal crime, Susan." Nor was murder. "The locals have jurisdiction."

"Quit talking to that Denver cop. What's his name, Johnson?"

I didn't tell her that.

"Never forget your friends, Paul. If there's one thing I've learned in Washington, it's—"

"—get a dog?"

"What?"

"Sorry, I'm in a bar. Good night, Susan."

Chapter Twenty-One

The combo plate was a salute to the Mexican flag. The burrito and enchiladas were striped red and green, and the tacos were slathered with sour cream. Paul draped his suitcoat over the back of his chair, tucked his tie into his crisp white dress shirt, and dug in. Special Agent Slatkin passed him the pozole.

"They soak the hominy in lye, Paul. You can't get food like this in D.C."

"Damn right."

The taqueria was way out on Colfax, deeper into East Bumblefuck than the local FBI fortress itself. For the Feds after 9-11, downtown offices no longer sufficed; the towering fence, colossal floodlights, and pervasive cameras made the new Denver headquarters look like a maximum-security prison. When Slatkin suggested lunch off-site, Paul offered to buy. As temporary license plates started outnumbering permanent tags, neon signs gave way to hand-painted block-lettered ones, and holes in the wall began touting catfish hotlinks, he knew he was being pimped. But dives were his kind of place. He reached for the menudo.

"You like cow's stomach?" Slatkin said doubtfully.

"When it's this tender." The chile was gelatinous from pork neck bones. "What's in the red sauce, ground coffee?"

Slatkin threw up his hands and surrendered to the menudo. As he slurped, the consternation on his face slowly turned to unalloyed delight.

"Tell me about the Petrosian case," Paul said. "You were

the lead agent, right?"

Slatkin grimaced. "It was supposed to be a slam-dunk seizure under the Trading with the Enemy Act."

"The case went sideways?"

"Fiasco start to finish. I warned them not to file it."

Paul ordered Coronas, and Slatkin continued.

"We got a tip Petrosian was planning to smuggle in an antique Chinese vase. When it landed in Denver, he claimed he bought it in Taiwan from a family who said it was modern. We seized the vase and indicted him for a false Customs declaration. Then the fun began."

"Fun?"

"His lawyers had the U.S. Attorney on the ropes from day one. Customs regs unconstitutionally vague, improper seizure, violation of Fifth Amendment, yada yada. The corker came first day of trial."

The waiter slammed two cold cans of Corona on the table. As Paul popped the tab and brought his can to his mouth, foam spurted up his nose and down his chin. He pulled the sweaty can back just in time to avoid staining his tie and shirt.

"Our expert was from Harvard," Slatkin said. "He said the vase was Qing Dynasty."

Paul's nose tickled from the beer. When was the last time he drank from a shaken can? It reminded him of the time he stuck a Mentos tablet in his old man's Coke.

"And?"

"He walks into court and looks at the defense table. 'Rosie!' he cries."

"He knew Petrosian?"

"Harvard classmates. Rosie has a PhD in art history."

"Shit."

"Experts pull their opinions from their ass," Slatkin groused. "Had a fraud case once—"

"What happened next?"

"'Rosie's the *real* expert,' our guy says. 'If he says it's modern, who am *I* to disagree?' Case didn't even reach the jury. The U.S. Attorney blamed us, then bitched about being micromanaged from D.C." Slatkin smiled with grim satisfaction. "He slunk back to Washington, but we tied that vase up in so much red tape Rosie had to climb up his own ass to see it again."

Paul signaled the waiter for another beer. "Is Rosie connected?"

"To organized crime?" Slatkin laughed with real amusement. "If he was, we wouldn't have screwed around with a Customs violation. We would've filed a RICO."

Paul was disappointed and relieved. The Armenian was a long shot, but you had to be thorough. That left Nick Lang and whatever friend of Jay Kurtz's Johnson scared up. Was that goose chase any wilder than Lily's theory?

"What do you know about art forgers?" he asked Slatkin.

Slatkin wiped his mouth. "Bunch of losers who can't sell their work."

"Any on your radar lately?"

"Nope."

Now he couldn't even take her to a steakhouse. Just one more loose end.

"I heard Kurtz tipped off Customs."

"So they say."

"Why would the Justice Department—"

"You'll have to ask the prosecutor. Or that gal from D.C. who had it in for Rosie. She pushed us to file, then micromanaged the case."

"Gal?" Paul said.

"Susan Grace."

———

"Did you arrest Jay Kurtz's friend?" Susan Grace asked that night.

"Not yet." *Careful now.* "I have another lead. Does Anton Petrosian ring a bell?"

"Petrosian... I don't think so."

"A defendant in a smuggling case twenty years ago." He waited. "George Kurtz tipped Customs off."

"What an odd coincidence!"

Coincidence, my ass.

"And you think this Petrushkin killed George. Who came up with that lead? Johnson, or your other friend?"

Does she mean Slatkin—or Lily?

"Local scuttlebutt," he said. "Johnson isn't in the loop."

"Let's keep it that way."

"I wondered about a mob connection. Armenians are tough—"

"Drop it, Paul."

"Pardon?"

"You've got the burglar. If it's smuggling you want, a joint task force in Seattle is investigating antiques from China..."

Or should we say Taiwan.

"... more suited to your talents. One call to the Director and you'll be heading it."

"How thoughtful of you, Susan."

She laughed. "One day his job will be yours."

Chapter Twenty-Two

"Don't play with that, Ollie!" Margo called out.

They sat on a bench in City Park, watching Margo's seven-year-old daughter examine a glob of goose poop in a puddle of mud. Olivia prodded the poop with her tiny Ugg. Mud splattered her white leggings, stopping short of her ballerina skirt.

"Mommy, the poop's green!"

Margo rolled her eyes at Lily. Once or twice a month she had Saturday morning off, and while Margo's son was at hockey or Little League, they took Olivia to the playground. As usual, they'd stopped on the way for lattes and one pink-frosted donut with sprinkles. Lily remembered the day Olivia was born, and the first time she looked up and recognized her.

"Don't the monkey bars look like fun, Ollie?" Margo said. Olivia twirled in her ballerina skirt and was off to the slides. "I can't get her out of a dress," she muttered with unmistakable pride. "What have I done wrong?"

"Not a damn thing. You're the best mother I know."

A peacock screeched from the zoo next door. Would they have time to take Olivia to see the baby giraffe? As they sipped their coffee, watching her and enjoying the sun, Lily remembered other Saturdays. Margo almost read her mind.

"Remember that bond lawyer who made us work weekends, just because he could?" They'd sworn they'd never do that when they made partner.

"What happened to him?"

"Died reading a trust indenture."

"Jeez!" *Paul saved me from that.*

Margo's voice softened. "Miss it?"

"No—yeah, maybe a little." She'd driven fifty miles to that client's bank, just to make sure it was real. That meant something, didn't it?

"The firm would take you back in a heartbeat. We still talk about that painting, you know."

"The Schiele?" Lily almost laughed. What would they say if they knew what she and Paul did on the conference room table afterwards? Not even Margo knew that.

"You're a role model for a generation of associates..." Margo insisted.

Sleeping with an adversary, then drowning my heartache with the married head of Litigation who had hair plugs?

"...really belong at the museum?"

"I love art, Margo, just not the business of it." *I hired you despite the Schiele, not because of it.* "And speaking of business—"

"Look, Mommy!" Olivia flung her arms in the air and flew down the slide.

"I'll never get those leggings clean," Margo despaired. "How's your new guy?"

"I honestly don't know what to make of him."

"Meaning?"

Lily hesitated. Maybe it was just an off-color joke, a clumsy line. "A Degas ballerina turned him on, Margo. He's unbelievably horny, or—"

"Jesus, Lily!" Margo laughed. "What rock have you been living under? Thirty-something guys these days don't know how to act around women."

"Maybe that's it..."

"You're a hot older babe, of course he's trying too hard. Name me one guy who doesn't overcompensate."

Paul. He doesn't even have to try.

Olivia ran up with a dandelion. "Make a wish, Lily, and blow!"

"I wish every Saturday was this one."

Olivia held the dandelion, and Lily blew. The fluff flew away, sparkling in the sun. Olivia ran off.

"That FBI man broke your heart," Margo said, "but enjoy this one while he lasts." She gave her a squeeze, and Lily hugged back. "Speaking of the energizer bunny, I found out more about that suit against Kurtz. It's a patent for a long-life battery."

Kurtz's murder. She should be focusing on his enemies, not going down a rabbit hole with Caillebotte or ruminating over her own problems with men. "Give me the *Cliff's Notes* version."

"Kurtz promised to use the battery in his drills. He buried the patent instead."

Buying a company for its crown jewel was standard practice. Sometimes burying the jewel was the end game. "So?"

"Most fossil fuels are used in cars," Margo said. "A long-life battery that really works would be the death knell for an oil-and-gas guy like Kurtz. The inventor sued. Kurtz and Mr. Wonderful were driving him into the ground."

"Who is he?"

"I'll find out."

Another dead end—good thing I didn't tell Paul.

"Big plans tonight?" Margo said.

"Dinner at my dad's. I'm introducing him to the little engine that could."

Olivia was at the swings. "Push me, Mommy!"

Margo left her bag and went to her daughter. She grabbed the swing and did a huge pullback.

Not like those Saturday walks when I was a kid.

Olivia shrieked with delight as she dipped and swung through the air.

Chapter Twenty-Three

Lily snipped chives and basil from the patch by the back porch. Through the bungalow's windows came laughter and the scents of garlic and Bolognese sauce. She'd made the lasagna with ground veal, the way her dad liked it, and the double batch would give him plenty of leftovers. The Franciscan ware in the sideboard would finally be used. When she was a child, how its hand-glazed apples, moss-colored leaves and molded stems enthralled her! Another burst of laughter, more raucous. Dave must be telling jokes.

For a know-it-all who shunned alcohol, her dad wasn't a bad host. He and Dave had picked up a couple of bottles of red on their way back from Black Hawk. Nick had brought two dozen roses, and his debut with her dad seemed to be going well. Back in the kitchen she searched for a knife to mince the shallot. Even her dad's cleaver was nicked and dull....

"This one." Nick selected a paring knife and tested it on his finger.

"That won't cut butter."

"Does your dad have a sharpener? No, of course not."

In the cupboard he found a chipped mug. Turning it upside down, he placed the paring knife's blade at a thirty-degree angle to the ceramic ring at the bottom. He drew the blade against the grain towards him, then tested its sharpness. "Patience, patience..." he murmured, doing it three more times. "Voilà!"

"You learn that in Boy Scouts?" Maybe that explained his

skill set and randiness.

"I was an Eagle Scout, and I grew up in a house with coffee cups and no knife sharpener."

"You sure know your way around a kitchen. Did your mom—"

"It was just my old man and me."

She gave Nick a hug. Smiling, he peeled and minced the shallot. She took the lasagna from the oven. Cheese and sauce bubbled, and the aroma was heavenly. He carried it to the dining room. "Ta-dah!" he cried.

"To the Degas ballerina!" Dave raised his tumbler. "And her savior, Lily. A true cause for celebration."

"A milestone for Amy, too," she said. "She's helping me revarnish it."

"Sweet," Nick said.

"Amy or the ballerina?" Dave winked slyly. He was gauging her dad's reaction to her new beau, and she braced for an evening of innuendos.

"How was Black Hawk?" she asked.

"I thought I was a gambler," Dave said, "but Harry taught me a thing or two."

Her dad's eyes gleamed. How much had he taken Dave for? She served the lasagna to *oohs* and *ahs*.

"You have a system, Mr. Sparks?" Nick asked.

Tell him to call you Harry.

"It's called using your eyes," he replied. "A postman does more than deliver mail."

Nick recovered nicely. "Isn't gambling an art?"

"Better than a damn science."

Uh-oh.

Dave jumped in. "Scientists aren't all bad, Harry. We chemists deal with physical matter, much the way a mailman—"

"We don't deal with particles. We deal with the public."

This would be so much easier if he drank! A mailman, a chemist, and an engineer walk into a bar... Lily giggled, breaking the tension, and passed the bread again. Black Hawk had given her dad an appetite, or was it the guests at his table? Dave threw the next punch.

"Engineers take things apart and fix what isn't broken.

Whereas chemists—"

"—ask why but can't do anything about it," Nick said. Color had risen in his cheeks, and there was no trace of that golly-gee-whiz Eagle Scout now. Unlike the other night in the lab, it was kind of a turn-on. She squeezed his leg.

Dave opened the second bottle of wine. "A chemist creates pigments."

"Who cares what paint's made of?" Nick said. "I know how to use it."

"Touché!" she cried.

The conversation turned to sports and politics, hot buttons at any other table. She cleared the dishes and made coffee.

"You're a student of art?" Dave was asking Nick.

"I liked the Samurai exhibit."

"Weapons don't belong in an art museum," Dave said.

"That exhibition creeped me out," she said, hoping to deflect another argument by passing around the biscotti and sorbet. "Not just the swords. Those four Samurai behind the velvet rope—"

"But aren't the masks great?" Nick said. "Even a chemist—"

"Science is overrated," her dad decreed, "and collecting is a pile of junk."

———

"Your dad's something else," Nick said as he was leaving.

She laughed. "He's harmless."

"I wish he was my old man."

"Really?"

"At least he's sober. How old were you when your mom died?"

"Five," she said.

"I know how that is. Never got over her, did he?"

"Pretty sharp for an Eagle Scout..."

"You forgot to dust the salad plates."

"I'm lucky to have them." Thank God her dad missed the gold compact when he threw out the rest of her mom's stuff. But Nick understood. She gave him an enthusiastic kiss.

"Tomorrow night?" he said.

———

"I'm worried about Harry," Dave said as he got into his pickup truck.

She stiffened. "Something happen in Black Hawk?"

"No, but with his leg he shouldn't be climbing a ladder."

She'd seen it against the garage, with the can of paint. "Dad's pretty nimble."

"It's more than that," he said. "When's the last time a plumber or electrician was here?"

"The toilets flush and the lights work...."

"I'm no *engineer*, but appliances and connections wear out. And with that McMansion next door, anything can happen." They gazed at the faux Mediterranean monstrosity with turrets on the corner lot.

"At least he'll have a neighbor." But not one like Walt.

Dave shook his head. "People no longer take pride in their work, Lily. You don't know how those sewer lines were installed."

"They were inspected."

"By experts?"

She patted his hand. "You've done wonders for him, Dave. He's lucky to have you as a friend."

He cranked the ignition and shifted into reverse. "At least check that stove!"

Chapter Twenty-Four

Vintage Antiques had survived gentrification and the wrecking ball. The used bookstores and sex emporia that were its neighbors on South Broadway were gone, but luckily not everyone preferred Ikea to nostalgia and junk. At Vintage, the cognoscenti could find whatever they were looking for.

The bell jingled as he entered the shop. Sweat, old shoes and manure hung in the air like dust. He breathed deeply, savoring this beloved haunt. Pile of junk, was it? What was a junk shop but a museum of unwanted objects in search of a connoisseur?

"Hello, Maude," he greeted the woman at the counter, "you look lovely today." Pin curls framed her face like grey pie crust. What would Rembrandt do with that face?

"Where've you been?" She offered him an underdone cookie from a paper plate. Crisco and coconut. He was a good customer.

"In the field. You know my work."

It was important; that's all she knew. She nodded, and he imagined her face fracturing into shards like a Picasso. "Anything exciting come in while I was gone?"

"That depends." She leaned forward and a riper odor wafted across the counter. The fan whirred, suffusing the air with her scent. He stepped back. "What're you looking for this time, more old books?"

Inspiration. "A good hoe, with a long handle and a strong blade."

"You're the tool expert."

His smile slipped. "Just an old hoe. The weeds have taken over."

She offered him another cookie. The coconut was greasy, and oil from the shortening dotted the dough's surface. Her face began to melt, elongating her chin until it stretched over the counter like a Dali clock. He declined the cookie with a regretful shake of his head. She leaned over the counter and winked. "You don't fool me."

"Beg pardon?"

"You're a collector."

He threw up his hands. "Busted!"

They shared a laugh.

"You know where the tools are. Holler if you need me."

He set off through the galleries of junk. At some point they'd been curated, but order and criteria had now succumbed to entropy. A shelf of herbs and spices, expiration dates decades old, hung over a bin overflowing with overalls and musty coats. In the next room a broken wheelbarrow leaned against a dinette with metal chairs. The table was set with an oilcloth and a dingy pitcher of plastic roses. *Imagine yourself in this kitchen. Hear the teakettle, smell the fresh-baked...*

Just like that, he was back home. A sink with filthy dishes, a refrigerator that stank and didn't keep his old man's six-packs cold. The cast iron pan on the gravy-stained stove was the only reminder of his mother. But he hadn't come to excavate memories.

Like a gopher's burrow, one airless room opened onto the next, each one's wares shoddier and more forlorn than the last. Display cases with costume jewelry and cheap watches, broken furniture giving way to unpaired shoes and rusted tools, an endless array of discards. But he was in no hurry.

He and his old man had trawled the junk shops near the farm town where he grew up. His old man collected tools and porn; you could find anything if you knew who to ask. Now, with the click of a mouse, he could summon things beyond the old man's wildest dreams. He'd been even more particular about his tools. They had to be wood or iron, honed razor sharp.

He passed a carton of knee-high rubber boots. His nostrils

twitched. Blood? No—an older memory. His old man worked the beet fields. He came home reeking of beer and the pulp's sickly stench, his hat and overalls and boots stained, his machete at his side. *Think you're too good for this, boy? I say what's good for you.* He'd escaped by graduating from school, getting a degree, and making far more of himself than his old man dreamed.

I got even with you for Junie. And I got even with Kurtz.

He thought of the night he finally met Kurtz. It was at the Fort Worth symposium for Energy Leaders of the West. At the reception at the Kimbell, Kurtz had held court, bragging about his expertise as a connoisseur and the paintings he owned. Touring the museum with Sully and drink in hand, he'd been just as Jay described: imperious as the Manchu Emperor, glittery eyes raping one masterpiece after another. He paused at *On the Pont de l'Europe.*

"What's this?" he asked Sully.

"A Caillebotte," Sully said.

Three men stood on a steel bridge. Two leaned against the railing with their backs to the viewer, one in a frock coat and top hat, the other in a derby and a canvas jacket, apparently watching the trains in the station below. The third man passed behind them before exiting the frame. What was striking was the anonymity—the furtiveness—of the man in the top hat. He stood too close to the fellow in the derby, and his hand was limp. Was he signaling?

Kurtz quickened beside him.

"Why haven't I seen him before?" Kurtz demanded.

"Most of Caillebotte's works are privately owned," Sully said.

"Get me one."

When the crowd thinned, he returned alone to *Pont.*

"Marvelous, isn't it?" the curator said. "The steel, those massive girders... Caillebotte painted another version. It, too, is called *Pont de l'Europe.* Come, I'll show you a print."

In the print, the top-hatted gent strolled the bridge with a lady carrying a parasol. But he was eying a youth in a canvas jacket who leaned on the railing—the same fellow in the Kimbell's version. No question which *Pont* came first, because Caillebotte's intent was clear: In *Pont One,* the gent ignored the lady because he was cruising the boy. He stood not on the bridge, but at the precipice of a decision. Would he choose her—or the boy? In *Pont Two*, he'd moved in. Caillebotte's two-act play perfectly captured the drama of coming alive. But no great act went unpunished. There was always a price to pay....

Sully returned and gave him and the curator his card. "If a Caillebotte comes on the market, call me."

He stayed in touch with Sully, who finally got him an audience with Kurtz. Kurtz was arrogant and crass. His Impressionists were stunning, but he was always looking for the next one. When he showed Kurtz one of his own paintings, Kurtz was dismissive—insulting. But he knew how to be patient, and his plan began to form. He knew just what glittering object would draw Jay's father to his fate....

Vintage's final room was an enormous trash heap. Stained sinks and tubs, broken chairs, bikes without wheels, the innards of two-burner stoves stacked ceiling high. Helpless to say no, the junk shop's curator had evidently given up. But these unwanted objects aroused him. *Take me,* they cried, *you know what I'm for!* He didn't need a leghold trap—not anymore, thank you very much!—but there were other prizes.

"Heavens!" Maude said when he returned. "What's that?"

"A beet topper." The hickory-handled machete had a foot-long steel blade with a pick at the end. "Haven't seen one in years."

"And what's this, a child's easel?"

A chalkboard one from the '40s, with a battered tin box of paints. The period was wrong, of course, but it reminded him of Brendan, his junior high classmate. And Junie, too. What a difference a little encouragement—recognition—would have made! Perfect eye or not, Lily was blind to that too. But he was about to open her eyes. He'd take what she cared about most and neutralize her with one elegant stroke. Too late to turn back? For her, but not for him. He, too, stood on the precipice Caillebotte captured so well.

"What on earth will you do with it?" Maude asked.

Pont One, or Two?

"The beet topper, or the easel?" he said.

"Either!"

He winked. "Like you said, I'm a collector."

Chapter Twenty-Five

The moment Lily entered her lab Monday morning, she knew something was dreadfully wrong. Amy leaned over the heat vacuum table, hands fluttering helplessly. The Objects Conservator and her assistant huddled behind her, as if afraid whatever was on the tarp might be infectious. Gina clutched her chest to stop herself from physically exploding.

Lily set down her backpack and slowly approached. Amy mutely turned to her, eyes wide as a lamb's. The Objects Conservator stepped back to make room. She looked down at the table. There lay the ballerina, but not the one she'd left on Friday.

The dancer's velvet surface had grown a glassy skin. The gold was gone from her tutu, now a garish rose instead of shell pink. Her satin toe shoes were rayon, the dance floor as glossy as a basketball court. And her hair—it was brass.

Worst of all, the composition no longer made sense. Instead of lit from the side, it seemed to be illuminated by a floodlight. The floor predominated, the ballerina was flattened, the illusion of depth was destroyed. As her eye struggled to find a way in, Lily's stomach heaved.

My poor ballerina! Did I bring you back to life to suffer this?

"What happened?" she said.

"I—" Amy began.

Lily had spent almost every waking hour of the past six weeks with the Degas. With each stroke of her swab she'd asked what the artist had intended. Each new revelation had brought greater admiration for Degas and affection for his girl in satin slippers.

"Where were you?" Gina's fury had found a voice and a target bigger than a lamb.

She'd stopped to feed Jack after leaving Nick's. "In my office," she told Amy. "Now."

"Stay right where you are," Gina ordered.

"Tell me what happened," Lily said.

"I came in over the weekend. I wanted to surprise you…"

You certainly did.

"…so I put it in the spray bath."

Lily struggled to stay calm. The canvas was especially thirsty after being cleaned, and the new varnish had sunk into the paint. The color was permanently changed. "We talked about spot-varnishing, Amy, and time to cure." Amy quickly glanced at Gina. "What varnish did you use?"

Now Amy looked her straight in the eye. "Matte, of course."

Bullshit. "You loaded the spray yourself?"

"Well, I—" she couldn't risk another glance at Gina— "I checked the code. Matte, not shiny."

"You tested it before you sprayed?" But it didn't matter. For the ballerina it was too late.

Gina quivered with triumph. Amy hung her head. She was young, she'd survive…. This was crazy. No conservator—no artist—would deliberately destroy a masterpiece.

"It's my responsibility," Lily said.

Gina smiled. "Sadly, I agree. I've spoken to Michel. He wants your resignation."

Even Amy looked shocked. Lily's colleagues stared at their feet. Budgets were being cut and Gina had Michel's ear.

I'm not taking this lying down. "The painting can be salvaged."

"Not by you," Gina replied. "Don't look so surprised— you've been on thin ice…"

This wasn't just about the Degas. It was because of Paul. Michel knew she was looking into the case, that she suspected *Seven* was connected to Kurtz. But the sheer wantonness of the ballerina's destruction felt strangely familiar. Like rendering a man into a landscape, a grotesque mockery of art.

It's what the killer did to Kurtz.

"Michel wants your resignation on his desk on Friday," Gina said.

Chapter Twenty-Six

The Ritz-Carleton lobby buzzed with women in chic frocks and men in blazers and designer loafers. The wall art was upscale hotel moderne but the floral arrangements were spectacular. Trying not to feel outclassed in her sneakers and jeans, Lily approached the reservation desk. The clerk's name tag said Sherri. She was as young and fresh as Amy. Would Amy get a promotion, an offer to join Gina's staff?

Lily pasted on a smile. "You have a guest named Paul Riley. Is he in his room?"

Sherri showed her teeth. "It's not our policy to divulge—"

Damn—another Amy. Lily made her smile as disarming as she could. "Of course not, Sherri, that would be unprofessional." She shrugged helplessly. "But you know guys. I forgot what time I'm meeting Paul, and he'll kill me if I'm late. Can you ring his room?"

Sherri winked and punched his number. "I'm afraid he's out. Want me to try the spa?"

"No thanks, Sherri. I'll wait."

Lily stationed herself on a banquette with a view of the door. She'd left two messages for Paul on his cell. When he didn't return them she gambled he was in town. It seemed crazy to link the Degas to Kurtz, but the ballerina's destruction felt like a second murder. She pictured Kurtz's claw-like hands, the sightless eyes in his brilliantined head. He and the dancer had been transformed into zombies. The walking dead of art.

A private van pulled up to the valet stand. Guests with

champagne flutes and Rockies caps tumbled out. With tonight's double-header and a stretch of home games scheduled, die-hard fans were celebrating early. She rose and paced the lobby. What did she expect from Paul, that he'd believe her because he'd once loved her? She had no Plan B.

She went to the concierge's desk. This girl's name was Tammy.

"I'm meeting Paul Riley for dinner, Tammy, but I forgot what time."

Lucky you, said Tammy's look. He'd impressed both clerks. By his generous tips, or that killer physique? Tammy looked over at Sherri, who nodded. She tapped at her machine. "You're way early. Elway's at 7:30 for two."

"Thanks, Tammy. I'll wait."

It was 5:10, but she knew Paul. He was as fastidious about grooming as Jack. He'd go to his room to shower. For a hot date with Gina he might even warm up with a few laps in that damn pool....

"Lily?"

She looked up. Paul's suit made her even more conscious of her sneakers and jeans.

"You never got back to me on my leads," she said.

"Your friend Rosie was cleared."

"No dinner at a swank steakhouse for me." He pulled out his cell and scanned messages. Was he truly busy? Tammy and Sherri watched from their desks. "Can we go somewhere and talk?"

"My room?" Paul said. It must've sounded cold even to him, because he relented and sat. "I heard you got canned."

Gina told him. "That's not why I'm here."

"If there was anything I could do—"

"Find who killed Kurtz."

He shook his head in exasperation. "Gustave Caillebotte himself, or your forger?"

"You believe me!"

He smiled grimly. "You're still seeing Nick Lang?"

"Jesus, Paul! He's got nothing to do with this."

He stood. "I can't help you if you won't help yourself."

Their time together unspooled in her head. From that first moment in the senior partner's office when they were introduced, to the night in the conference room with the Schiele, to every hour they'd spent in the sack. Their epic arguments, from legal theory to the meaning of contemporary art, to what takeout place had the best Thai. He'd backed her up on the Schiele and gotten Elena's indictment dismissed. When did he turn into this stranger in a well-cut suit?

She reached for his hand.

"I know you, Paul. You're not afraid of the truth, and you don't walk away from a fight." He drew back and his eyes flashed with anger. "Don't you care who killed Kurtz?" He shook her off and turned to leave. "What the hell happened to you?"

"What gets us all, Lily. We grow up. As for what I'm really doing here," he said briskly, "tonight I have a dinner date. Tomorrow I'm wrapping up this case. Then I'll fly home to D.C."

"You'll let a killer walk."

He shrugged. "For your own good, Lily, let it go."

"Not till you do."

"I already have."

With those three words, her last hope died.

"Go home, lick your wounds, get drunk," he said. Nothing was worse than his pity. "You'll find another job. But stay away from Nick."

Chapter Twenty-Seven

Lily ordered another Snake Spit. Its name and the Rock Bottom Brewery said it all.

"At least wash that down with some wings," Margo said.

"You're the one who suggested this joint."

"I didn't know the Rockies—" A deafening cheer drowned her out. The pub was within sight of Coors Field and was packed with purple ball caps. "Be glad we scored a booth."

Tonight she would've met Margo in Timbuktu. As she was leaving the Ritz, Margo called and said she had something about the FBI. The good thing about drinking with her was she always had to go back to the office or home to her kids. But for once, neither of them was in a rush.

"How's the love of your life?" Margo asked.

"Gone."

"He quit docent training?"

"What?" *She means Nick.* "No, we're still hanging out."

"How was Saturday night?"

"He held his own against a mailman and a chemist."

"That doesn't sound sexy," Margo said.

"You should see him with a knife."

Margo squinted. "What's wrong, Lily?"

"Tell you later." *I'll have nothing but time.*

"Don't want to spoil the high?"

"Unfortunately, I'm stone sober."

A Rockies fan passed their booth with a pitcher of beer. Someone jostled his elbow, and beer sloshed all over Lily's hair.

You stinking putz!

"Sorry!" Grinning helplessly, he gave her his sweat-soaked ball cap. Before she could say anything, he disappeared into the crowd.

"And they say chivalry's dead," Margo said.

Lily jammed the cap on her head and surveyed the bar. The Rockies had won the first game. Rowdier fans were taking the place of the half-tanked ones leaving for the stadium. Why did Margo suggest meeting here?

"Why the cloak-and-dagger?" Lily said.

"This is the last time we'll talk."

Fuck Paul and the beer. She flagged a waiter. "You make a Manhattan?"

"Yeah. What's your pleasure?"

"Stranahan's. Make it a double and bring two."

Margo laughed. "I'm fine, Lily. I meant about Kurtz. I know why the FBI was called in."

The waiter brought their Manhattans and a platter of hot wings with blue cheese and buffalo sauce. Did Margo order them? The sauce was a neon orange slick. It gleamed like the ballerina's new hair.

"...worried about you, Lily. I've never seen you drink like this."

Only when I lose my job and am within a million miles of Paul.

"What about the FBI?" Lily said.

Margo leaned in closer. For the first time, she looked nervous. "Does Susan Grace ring a bell?"

"Sounds like a prostitute."

"A high class one. *Senator* Grace heads the Senate Committee on the Judiciary and the subcommittee on Crime and Terrorism."

"And?"

"She works with the FBI and oversees federal sentencing reform."

"So?"

"Kurtz needed her to eliminate penalties for environmental crimes. You did *not* hear this from me."

"So Kurtz was indicted..."

"He ran smack into an endangered species habitat. Who knew a Preble's meadow jumping mouse could shut down a major pipeline? Point is, she's up for reelection and can't afford a scandal over campaign contributions and a derailed indictment."

Is that what Paul meant by growing up?

Margo rummaged in her purse and came up with a small spray bottle. She spritzed it in her mouth before offering it to Lily. "Phil thinks I'm working late... Oh, I almost forgot." She reached in her purse again and pulled out a manila envelope.

"What's that?"

Margo hesitated, then gave it to her. "That lawsuit over the company Kurtz bought."

She looked at Margo blankly.

"The battery that'll bring the oil and gas industry to its knees," Margo reminded her. "Very hush-hush. The last motion was to seal the case." She zipped her purse and rose. "I mean it, Lily. If this gets out, I'm in deep shit." She bent to kiss her cheek. "Mmn. Beer and buffalo sauce and whisky. Want a lift?"

"Mr. Prius is parked out front. And he uses almost no gas."

Margo looked concerned. "I'll call you a cab."

Lily shook her head.

"You'll go straight home?" Margo insisted.

"Yeah."

———

Rockies double-headers brought the cops out in force, and the last thing she needed was a drunk driving arrest. She tossed Margo's unopened envelope in the Prius' backseat and closed her eyes. Paul and the Senator.

Slowly she counted to ten. Then she pulled out her cell and began googling.

Susan Grace. Lots of hits of a cougar in a power suit.

Senate Committee on the Judiciary. Susan Grace shaking hands with Kurtz on the U.S. Capitol steps, the same photo in the slide show at his memorial. Closer—but not what she was looking for. Rockies fans were streaming like lemmings from Coors Field to the bars downtown. A man banged on her window. He made a rude gesture possibly intended to persuade her to relinquish her parking space. *Piece of shit*

Prius, he mouthed. She ignored him.

Subcommittee on Crime and Terrorism + Paul Riley. Bingo. A shot of Susan Grace and her fair-haired boy. Was he her bag man, too?

Lily pulled from the curb and drove to the Ritz.

Chapter Twenty-Eight

Rockies cap pulled low, Lily hunched over Elway's bar. In the mirror she watched Gina and Paul. An attractive couple: he broad and fit in his fancy suit, she in a slinky black sheath with lace-capped shoulders. Their conversation looked spirited.

"Club soda, Miss?"

Lily nursed her whisky. They were finishing their steaks. No wine on the table.

"Perhaps some food?" the bartender said. "We don't usually serve at the counter, but the kitchen's open..."

"I won't be here that long."

Gina shook her head vehemently. Lover's spat? Paul signaled for the check, and without waiting rose and pulled out her chair. Gina took her time bending to retrieve her purse, displaying a skinny shank and a thigh pale as marble. He took her arm impatiently—almost a bum's rush. Now they were at the door to the lobby. Lily threw some cash on the bar, grabbed her backpack and intercepted them smoothly.

"Having fun your last night in town?" she asked Paul. Gina reared back. "We need to talk."

He gave Gina some money. "Take a cab. I'll call you later." Wide-eyed, Sherri watched from the reception desk. She reached for a phone—to call Tammy?

"Are you afraid of me?" Lily said.

"No. You're making a fool of yourself." He took her whisky glass and set it down. Locking her in a one-armed embrace, he dragged her to the elevator. "We're going to my room." He said it under his breath, but he was seething. "And you're going to keep your mouth shut until we get there."

He smiled at a well-dressed couple getting off the elevator. They looked at her and their faces froze. He used a key card for access to the eighteenth floor. She was silent until they entered his suite. He went into the bedroom.

"You lied to me," she called after Paul. "You're not here to solve Kurtz's murder. You're here to bury it."

He returned with a bathrobe. He threw it at her—hard. "Get in the shower."

"That some kinky shit you do with Gina—or Susan Grace?"

"We're not talking till you're sober." He pulled the Rockies cap from her head. With it came the stench of sweat and beer. "Jesus, Lily, is that buffalo sauce on your face?" He went into the bathroom and turned the shower on full blast.

"I don't want a shower." It came out like a child arguing with a parent.

"Of course not. You want to embarrass us both because you can't get what you really want."

"I want the truth." She sounded petulant, and her legs felt wobbly. Her nausea over the Degas returned. *Don't you dare puke now.* She sank onto the couch.

"You and your perfect eye," he said. "The only reality is what you see."

She struggled to focus. "You came here to dump the case."

"Missed your calling, Lily. You're one helluva prosecutor, jury and judge." He bent to untie her sneakers.

"Kurtz gave her money."

"The Senator has nothing to do with this."

"It wasn't a burglar."

"Yeah, I know." He stripped off her socks. "It was an art forger."

"He wants us to admire him, to recognize his genius." *Sjostrom said it so much better!* "And he destroyed the Degas."

"Why would Kurtz's murderer destroy a Degas?" Paul said.

"To get me fired."

He laughed. "There are easier ways to do that. You know how crazy you sound?"

Now the whole thing seemed preposterous. Had she succumbed to the worst kind of tunnel vision, fallen into the most elementary trap? Paul shook his head. "You're a lawyer, Lily. You think an art forger murdered Kurtz? Prove it."

"But—"

"Get in that shower or I'll throw you in."

"I don't want a shower," she repeated. "I want—"

"The truth?" He'd never sounded so furious. "What truth is that, Lily? Who killed Kurtz, or how you can love someone who's too selfish and rotten to love you back? Go ask your lying father."

"My dad?"

Paul dragged her to the bathroom and pushed her into the shower stall. He turned on the water all the way. Icy pellets hit her face like a shotgun blast. Her throat closed. Her chest seized and she couldn't breathe. She was trapped in a frozen lake, back on that camping trip with her dad and Walt after her mom died.

They'd told her to wait while they cut a hole in the ice to fish, but she followed them onto the lake. When she stepped off the bank, the shimmery glaze at the edge shattered like spun glass—*pop, pop, crack!* Before she could scream she was dragged under by an iron grip. It hauled her to the thicker ice at the middle of the lake. Everything went milky like bone. She looked up. Through the translucent crust she saw diamonds and stars. Then they dimmed and it was so cold.... Suddenly another hand, Walt's big warm one, crashed through and yanked her free.

You're okay.

Coughing and sputtering, she jerked back from the showerhead and leaned against the wall. When she could breathe again, she turned off the cold water and turned on the steam. She stripped off her top and jeans and dropped them by the drain. Sinking to the floor in her wet panties and bra, she began to cry. The ballerina, Amy, getting fired—*Paul.*

Her hair was gritty and stank of beer. In the steam she smelled sweat. Not even her own. It came from the Rockies cap. She scrubbed at the stickiness on her cheek, but the foreignness clung. *I hate chicken wings.* Slowly she got to her feet. She wriggled out of her panties and bra and turned her face up. Like a big warm hand, the steam enveloped her.

When she got out of the shower and went into the bedroom, the robe was on the neatly turned-down bed along with a fancy chocolate. *Where is he?*

The door to the outer suite was closed. She put her ear to it.

Gone again.

She left her clothes on the bathroom floor and crawled into bed.

Chapter Twenty-Nine

Paul was furious at her and even angrier at himself. *Why did I get her into this?*

While she slept it off, he gave her clothes to the concierge and spent the night on the couch. Not wanting to wake her, he'd foregone his own shower and a clean suit. Her going off the deep end about Kurtz's killer being a forger risked screwing up his investigation. But in her current state, she was no threat to anyone—for once, not even to herself. He hoped she had one helluva hangover.

Johnson offered him another cup of coffee. The same slop at cop shops everywhere.

"Rough night?" Did his rumpled suit make Johnson an expert in that, too? He didn't know the half of it.

"Yeah." Lily was right. He'd been climbing the FBI ladder, but not so long or fast that he'd forgotten his job. Sure as hell wasn't turning a blind eye to a murderer to close out a case so his mentor wasn't embarrassed.... *Focus.* "Can we get into Nick Lang's garage? There's a reason he padlocks it and covers the window. He has a gas delivery system somewhere."

Johnson looked doubtful. "Why would Kurtz let him in?"

"I don't know." He was in no mood to be cross-examined. "Maybe he brought beer."

"Beer?"

"Never mind."

He shouldn't have called her father a liar. It was a cheap shot, but he knew more about Harry Sparks than she did;

he'd made it his business to know. He'd pleaded with Gina to save her job, but it was like squeezing honey from a stone. Why did she have to poke a sharp stick in Gina's eye? How could someone so smart be so emotionally blind? But it was his own fault. He'd put her at risk in the first place and everything he'd done since had made it worse. Johnson seemed amused.

"Here's how it works, Paul. You bring me probable cause—"

"Have you interviewed Angela Kurtz? That feud with Lang wasn't just a lawsuit. She'll tell you how bitter—"

"—and I ask a judge for a warrant. It can't be that different in D.C."

Johnson was right. He needed more.

"Have you thought of flowers?" Johnson said.

"Flowers?"

"For the little blonde. And it wouldn't kill you to shower."

———

She awoke alone in his bed. A peek through the crack in the door to the outer room assured her he was gone, if he'd been there at all. Staggering to the bathroom, she hoped he put out the *Do Not Disturb* sign. The last people she needed to answer to were the Ritz's housekeeping staff. She turned on the faucet in the sink, then looked in the mirror.

Is that me?

It was like glancing at a store window and realizing the stranger looking back was you. Not so much the grey strands at her temple as her haggardness. Her eyes were hollow. The red stain on her lips accentuated fine lines around her mouth. Like cracks in a painting; once you noticed them, they were everywhere. She touched her cheek, trying to superimpose the unsmiling blonde stranger standing at the bungalow door with the suitcase.

I'm older than mom ever was.

She turned the water on in the sink until it ran cold. She drank some and rinsed her mouth. Paul's shaving gear was set out neatly on the marble counter. He used to line it up exactly that way in her bathroom at the condo, but the Remington single-blade and drugstore shaving cream were now a silver-handled razor and a badger hair brush. Did she really think he'd protect her by believing in her, and keep doing it for ten years and from 2000 miles away? That was as crazy as hoping to catch a glimpse of her mom by snapping her compact open fast enough. Or that if she looked hard enough at the swirling galaxy and crystal stars on the lid she'd see her there. Only in a fairy tale, and certainly not after last night.

Last night.

She had a dim memory of Paul throwing her in the shower and her falling through the ice in that lake when she was a kid—that old monster. Muzzy as she'd been, she remembered every word he said. *Deluded and pathetic, so incompetent you deserved to lose your job*—oh, and her dad was a liar. *You're a lawyer, Lily. If you think a forger killed Kurtz, prove it.* She didn't know what to believe anymore. And what did it matter now? After yesterday she had no job, no future as a conservator, not even her dignity. Whoever killed Kurtz and destroyed the ballerina had won.

The marble counter had a dizzying array of luxury products. With a pre-moistened towelette meant to spare the hotel's linen the ravages of lipstick and mascara, she scoured the red from her lips. The towelette emitted the faint but familiar chemical scent of the Baby Wipes she used on Jack while he convalesced. They were soft and emollient, gentler than the solvent for the poor ballerina, and kinder than she herself deserved. But she couldn't stand here all day feeling sorry for herself.

Get your shit together and go before he comes back.

Someone—a maid?—had brought in her makeup bag. Lily dumped its contents onto the counter. Compact, lipstick, lipliner… The Ritz had a fancy magnifying mirror with a high-powered bulb. She began putting on her lipstick and stopped. In the unforgiving light the pomegranate looked garish, like the ballerina's high-gloss varnish. She rubbed it off with the towelette. It was time to consider a softer shade, a matte pigment, maybe a deep rose? Not the all-day kind that dried out, but a rich creamier one.

You survived that monster in the lake.

Could she find a job, make a new life? A small museum

somewhere might be hiring, or a private collector. She scrubbed off the last of the pomegranate. Her face was naked without it, but the eyes that stared back weren't quite so hollow as before. The woman in the mirror was starting to look familiar. *You must believe in something bigger than yourself, Lily.* She'd been wrong about Paul, and Amy—so much for her eye being perfect. What made her so sure about the connection between *Seven* and Kurtz?

Go back to the painting.

If Kurtz was murdered by a forger, as Sjostrom suggested, and he modeled the murder on *Seven*, did that mean the painting was forged? If *Seven* was forged, the forger was good enough to fool Sully and Michel. He was sitting pretty because there were so few Caillebottes to compare it to. But if she wasn't perfect, he wasn't either. Somewhere he slipped up. She still had a brain and an eye—not perfect, but good enough.

You don't have to be perfect to solve Kurtz's murder.

She looked in the mirror again. Her eyes were already brighter, her face not so sallow. She ran her fingers through her hair, brushing it from her forehead. The white scar gleamed. Something inside her stirred. Did it matter what Paul or anyone else thought? The stirring grew insistent, like a wisdom tooth working its way through a calcified gum. What did she believe?

The bastard who forged Seven *and killed Kurtz somehow destroyed the Degas.*

She couldn't explain it yet, much less prove it. But if that was true, and he did it to get her fired, she was partly responsible for the ballerina's death. If not for her, the little dancer would have been reborn. Stepping onto the stage and taking her bow before the world. Innocent, unsullied, pure. She shook her head.

No. This is on him.

Who would stop him, who would make him pay? Not the FBI. But the woman in the mirror knew the answer. The force within her erupted, catapulting up and smashing through gum and ice and bone.

I'll get him myself.

———

Her clothes were laundered and neatly folded on the credenza in the suite's outer room. Even the Rockies cap was clean and pressed. She threw it in the waste basket. Paul had left no note. Too hung over to be tempted by the orange juice and croissants on the sideboard, she grabbed her backpack and took the elevator to the lobby. Sherri and Tammy were off duty, but she avoided the reception desk and concierge stand. Outside she tried to remember where she'd parked. If the Prius hadn't been towed, she'd run up a fortune in tickets.

"Taxi, miss?" the valet said.

"No, thanks. I have a car."

He took a key from the stand. "I'll have your Prius pulled around."

"But I didn't—"

"The gentleman took care of it."

His last gallant act.

———

At her condo she apologized to Jack. Louise had been taking him out onto the balcony in the afternoon, and his coat was glossy and thick again. She opened the sliding door and watched him warily circle the tomato plants until he found his patch. What was it about the killer, that made him destroy what she loved? And if he went after Jack and the Degas, why stop there?

Hands shaking, she rummaged in the pantry for cat treats. There were the Baby Wipes for Jack's other eight lives. Remembering the Ritz's towelette, she read the label. The only limit to their use seemed to be the imagination, but she'd never apply those chemicals to an infant. Formaldehyde—did she really wipe that on Jack? Hydroquinone—benzene, wasn't that a carcinogen? And phthalates, an industrial solvent. The packaging was as deceptive as the name. Maybe Margo was right and she could go back to law. Shuddering, she threw the wipes in the trash.

She changed into a silk T-shirt and fresh jeans and hung the clothes she'd been wearing at the very back of her closet. Feeling better, she washed her face properly and applied a little lip gloss. She had no job, and her career was probably over. At the close of business on Friday, her resignation would be on Michel's desk. Paul was right. If she believed *Seven* was forged and the forger killed Kurtz, she had to prove it herself.

She brought Jack in and bolted the balcony door. She kissed his head and whispered in his ear. "I won't let him hurt you again." *Or me.*

She had no more time to look. Now she had to *see*.

Chapter Thirty

Fanning herself with her boarding pass, Lily tipped the cabbie who dropped her at the Kimbell Art Museum in Fort Worth. She grabbed her backpack and approached the vaulted entryway. The real gem in this sky-lit jewel box of Asian and European art was Caillebotte's *Gennevilliers Plain, No. Three*. And having gone to graduate school with the Kimbell's director of conservation, she had an entrée. When she'd called Sean and said she was coming, he didn't ask why. Now she went directly to his studio.

"Lily!" They embraced.

Sean's atelier was flooded with natural light from a glass wall facing north, prized for the soft, cool glow which bathed a room throughout the day. An open floor with tables and tall easels and wheeled stands for tools and paints added to the airiness and transparency. The glass wall overlooked an interior courtyard with potted trees. The Kimbell's conservators were surrounded by nature and visitors could see in. Maybe someday…

"You made out like a pirate, Sean."

With his blond goatee and gold earring, Sean looked like his ancestors must have been buccaneers. But blood had thinned, and the image was undercut by his gentle North Carolina drawl. They spent a few minutes catching up on friends and reminiscing about conservation school's holy trinity: art history, studio and chemistry. Unlike her, he'd aced chem.

"You really run this place?" she said.

"With an assistant. The beauty of a small shop."

How liberating not to share a lab with other conservators! Each specialty had its idiosyncrasies. Paper was anal, Textiles worse. Objects was the division of pots and pans; she hid her good brushes from them because they were messy and careless with tools. The Kimbell evidently understood painting was the highest form of art, but she wasn't here for a job.

"How's Denver?" he asked.

"Not great."

He squinted. "Ready to jump ship?"

"You mean walk the plank."

Lily gave him an abbreviated version of the Degas fiasco. He knew better than to ask why she took the hit for Amy.

"Did you like private practice?" she asked.

"A burnout." Before the Kimbell, he'd handled a San Francisco newspaper tycoon's collection. "Worse, you can't control what happens to the art. At a museum you're custodian of a collection...." He looked at her quizzically. "But that's not why you came."

"I want to see Caillebotte's *No. Three*."

"Anything to do with the Degas?" He took her silence for his answer. "Funny you should ask. I was just about to take *Three* down to inspect the lining..."

Sean brought *Three* to the studio and set up lamps. It was the same size as *Seven*, but less dramatic: plowed golden fields, a smattering of wildflowers, an off-center vanishing point where field met sky. No little man with a hat. Sean was quick on the uptake; she didn't need to tell him she suspected *Seven* was forged.

"No painting's a hero to its conservator," he said. "Like butlers, we have our doubts. But I've seen your Caillebotte."

"And?"

"Nothing leaped out. What bothers you?"

Kurtz was murdered because of it and the killer may be coming after me.

"The provenance doesn't add up, Sean. It's based on a nonexistent study in Caillebotte's sketchbook and a letter to Monet."

His eyes narrowed. "The two artists did correspond."

"The only person who claims he saw the letter is dead."

"So your forger—if it *is* forged—was clever." He chuckled. "But no museum will disavow a Caillebotte because of a lost letter and a mistake about a sketchbook."

"How do you know yours is real?" she countered.

"Aside from an unbroken chain of title going back to the Franco-Prussian War?"

Which they both knew ended before 1884, but why spoil the mood? If Sean said *Three* was real, he'd done his homework. She turned to the painting. *What am I looking for?* Something, anything that differentiated the two landscapes from each other. She pulled out her loupe and began examining *Three*.

Parallel lines with Filbert brush or palette knife—same as *Seven's*. Strong horizontal compositional line, wet-on-wet, multiple applications of paint. Was *Seven's* impasto this thick? Cross-hatching, scoring, dredging with stick. Poking brush against surface, laying tip on canvas and twisting. From Caillebotte's *tache*—his touch to the canvas—she could tell the size and shape of every brush he used. Sean was watching her intently.

"Think I'll go out for a smoke," he said casually, "if you don't mind being alone." He didn't smoke. "I'll be back in—" —he made a show of looking at his watch—"—say, eight minutes."

Touch all you want. He closed the door behind him.

Lily shut her eyes and ran her hands lightly over the canvas. A current ran from her fingertips to the soles of her feet.

Three was pliable and thickly textured, rough as a man's beard, with ridges like alpine peaks and twists and whorls and swales. One pinnacle was so sharp she drew back for fear of breaking it off. She recalibrated her touch, fluttering her fingers and flying over the painting's surface like a bird. *Caillebotte did this, this is real.* His *tache* told her precisely where in the painting she was: The clouds were nubby, the plow marks deeply scored, the grass moved. At the vanishing point she drew in her breath. *He marked it.* She felt each stroke, touched his soul on the canvas. Could a forger fake an artist's soul? If only Paul were here .... At the sound of a gentle cough, her eyes flew open.

"I'll have whatever you're having," Sean said.

She blushed.

"You can almost smell the sewage field from the Seine," he continued. "A truly underappreciated fertilizer, despite the methane."

She looked up. "Methane?"

"The main component of sewer gas."

Seven *didn't just inspire Kurtz's murder. The killer replicated it.*

"If you wanted to poison someone with methane, Sean, how would you do it?"

He stroked his goatee. "Victims usually die in their sleep. I'd use a canister and hose and wear a protective mask. Or rig something to explode. Why do you—"

"You said *Three* is lined."

He turned the painting over. A liner was a second canvas bonded to the reverse side of the original one to stabilize it. *Three*'s canvas was a fine linen—Caillebotte could afford the best—but it had started to fray. On the *verso*, the reverse side, Lily's trained eye easily picked up where the liner met the frayed edge. Like ironing on a Levi's patch, bonding one canvas to another required heat. Above 200 degrees, oil paint became malleable and the canvas could be flattened or acquire a new texture. *Three* hadn't met that fate.

"Who lined it?" she said.

"Dunno, but thank God he was careful."

He stroked the verso, inviting her to do so. Her fingers roamed it, memorizing the two weaves. Like the original canvas, this liner was linen, but significantly newer and more tightly woven. The difference in age between it and Caillebotte's canvas supported *Three*'s authenticity; lining or relining with materials of the same vintage as the original was a tip-off that a forger had tried to make it look old. But even big museums like hers didn't ordinarily examine liners. Not on Michel's watch.

She was dying to examine *Seven*. Unless she wanted to raise eyebrows by scanning her badge at the loading dock after the museum closed, she had to catch her plane. Sean looked disappointed.

"Surely you have time for *Pont de l'Europe*..."

She'd forgotten the Kimbell's more celebrated Caillebotte, but it was in Nick's catalog: The man in the top hat and lady with the parasol, strolling Paris's newly-built steel bridge over the Gare Saint-Lazare. If Kurtz's killer chose Caillebotte, maybe this wasn't about just one painting.

In the North Gallery, they waited for the crowd at *Pont* to disperse. Nearly twice the size of the canvases in the *Gennevilliers Plain* series, this Caillebotte was rendered in the cool blues and greys of the artist's cityscapes. She remembered the steel bridge over the train tracks. But here two men leaned against the railing while a third exited the frame.

"Where's the lady with the parasol?" she said.

"Ah! That's the bridge painting everyone thinks of," Sean said. "I call it Act One in Caillebotte's morality play. This is Act Two, what happened next."

Lily closed her eyes and summoned Act One. Top Hat was the leading man.

Details, please.

His hat and frock coat signified status and control. His companion with the parasol wore a fashionable hat and floor-length Edwardian dress with an hourglass silhouette. They appeared to be together. Was he Caillebotte, and she Charlotte Berthier? The youth at the railing with his back to them wore a rough canvas jacket. The dog in the foreground was a spaniel with white markings and silky red hair.

More.

Top Hat's chin bent towards the woman, but he was staring at the working-class boy. Despite his furtive bearing, something about Top Hat suggested he wanted to be noticed—to be recognized. Caillebotte had caught him at the brink, on the cusp of a life-changing decision.

Now the dog.

The spaniel trotted towards Top Hat, tail high in the universal sign of canine friendship. His coat was too fine for a stray and he seemed to know the man. But he was a side act. His hind paw was cut off by the frame.

What's hiding in plain sight?

Top Hat was torn between the woman and the boy. Which

way would he go? Lily opened her eyes and stepped closer to the Kimbell's denouement of the drama on the bridge. A security guard approached but Sean waved him back.

Trust your eye.

In Act Two—the Kimbell version—Top Hat had moved in. Was the boy in the canvas jacket a stand-in for the mannish Anne-Marie Hagen, the woman Caillebotte reinvented as Charlotte Berthier? The gent exiting the frame was also an aristocrat. All three men looked away from the viewer, as if they wished to be anonymous. Top Hat's expressiveness centered on his own right hand. Hanging limply from his tapered black coat, it was pale and hairless. The fingers curled like a baby's.

"Prostitution was rampant in Paris," Sean said. "Train stations were where men met."

Seven's man with the brimmed hat was rushing into the storm. Not to safety, but to the anonymity and danger of the trees. If Kurtz's murder was a morality play, the curtain rose on *Pont de l'Europe*. Did it fall on Kurtz, was *Seven* Act Three?

"Stay at my place tonight." Sean grinned wickedly. "I'll show you Fort Worth's version of the Gare Saint-Lazare…."

But she was rushing to a cab.

Chapter Thirty-One

When Lily's plane landed, the museum was closed. She badged in at the loading dock. Frank, the roly-poly Ops chief, was at his computer eating a meatball grinder.

"Working late, Ms. Sparks?"

I'll miss Frank and our morning coffee.

"I need to examine the Caillebotte on Level Six. Can one of your guys bring it to me?"

That solved three problems: disarming *Seven* without triggering an alarm, taking it down without Gina or Michel getting wind of it, and safely transporting it to her lab. Twenty minutes later, Caillbotte's masterpiece lay on the heat vacuum table's tarp.

Lily unscrewed it from the frame: an Eden frozen in eternity against the violence of the clouds, the moment before all was lost. But the time for illusions was past. She pulled out her loupe.

Composition first.

The man with the hat provided a dramatic focus Caillebotte's other landscapes lacked. Ignoring him for the moment, she transposed Kurtz's head onto the stand of trees. High-browed and aquiline, grimacing and imperious, with his thinning hair slicked to his skull and made black and glistening by the brilliantine the killer applied. A grotesque fit.

Brushwork.

A forger could match an artist's palette, but not his touch. The cross-hatching of the grasses resembled Caillebotte's technique in *Three*. In the foreground the artist had used wet-on-wet, painting on top of an existing layer before it dried. That let him mix his colors on the canvas and work more spontaneously. The overlaid cadmium and vermilion were saturated and brilliant. Atop a fluid layer, his brush could fly like the killer's knife.

Now the acid test.

Eyes closed, Lily ran her fingers lightly over the canvas. The clouds projected in rough, built-up layers, thicker and more textured than *Three*'s. Grasses moved in the wind, plow marks were as deeply scored. The poppies were painted with larger bristles but the same vigorous... *Look for the imperfection,* Paul had said a lifetime ago, *the tiny space that lets the painting breathe.* At the man with the hat, she paused. Did the stroke stiffen, or was it the urgency of an artist at the mercy of his muse?

The man doesn't fit.

Him scurrying into the storm gave the landscape a kind of randomness. Deliberate—and not subtle. Caillebotte's humility, or a forger's hubris? *You're a lawyer, prove it.* No matter what her gut said, she needed objective evidence.

Lily turned *Seven* over. Like *Three,* the canvas was lined. If the liner was added to strengthen the canvas, and not to make the painting appear older, it should be newer. Maybe even a synthetic.

Closing her eyes one last time, she ran her fingers over the verso and tried to find where canvas and liner met. The original was a fine, tight weave, the same expensive linen Caillebotte used for *Three*. She felt for subtle ridges, gently probing for roughness that indicated fraying.

What the hell?

Lily went back and forth between canvas and liner. Both were flat and smooth. Not from heat-bonding, but because they were the same weave. She opened her eyes to be sure. Canvas and liner didn't just feel the same; under the bright light they had the identical sheen.

The forger had made a mistake.

If only Paul were here!

Her eye still worked, she was right, he'd believe her now! But the feeling quickly died. Needing Caillebotte's Eden to be real had blinded her to the most obvious thing: he didn't paint figures in his landscapes.

She touched the canvas again, then jerked her hand back. What she'd felt wasn't Caillebotte's touch. It was the killer's. His vile triumph had reached through the linen and stained her. The little man would never reach shelter. He was Top Hat on the bridge. Rushing into the storm wasn't his fate. It was his punishment for hubris.

Call Paul.

She found her phone in her backpack and hit the speed dial.

Come on, answer...

"Lily?"

Nick stood at the door. Did they have a date tonight? He didn't know she'd gone to Fort Worth, or that she was fired. She slipped her cell in her pocket. "How'd you get in?"

"Scout's motto is *Be Prepared*." He held up his lanyard and ID. "I told Frank we had a hot date and showed him the photo from the other night."

"Photo?"

Nick scrolled through his phone to a shot of her in the bungalow's kitchen, bending to remove the lasagna from the oven. A candid but casual pose, as intimate as the ballerina and anonymous as the men in *Pont de l'Europe.* "Frank remembered your old man, so I showed him this too." Dave pouring wine and her father toasting with his water glass—a Spartan abbot and his bawdy monk. Like a good artist, Nick had caught something essential in them both. "I wish your dad liked me more."

"He gave you points for trouncing Dave."

"I guess.... You shouldn't be alone here at night."

He was right. The museum was a maze of walls that didn't meet and corridors that appeared to lead nowhere. The lab was particularly isolated. After dark, she had to feel her way down the hall, through two galleries and the elevator lobby, past a supply room and an electrical closet, just to reach the ladies' room. Apart from its double metal doors, the only access into the lab was the broom closet leading to the roof, and the freight elevators. When she worked late, she heard the elevators wheeze and groan and rattle through the shafts.

"I tried calling you," Nick said.

"I turned off my phone, but Ops knows I'm here."

"Look how easily I got in. Frank's a nice guy, but..." The museum's interior cameras had blind spots, including in the lab. When the lights were off, not even Ops could see. Lily followed Nick out. *Call Paul again, or try to reach Michel?*

"What's with the Caillebotte?" Nick said. The canvas lay face down on the heat vacuum table. Did Nick recognize its frame?

"Just looking for labels and stamps," she said, "clues to where it was while it was lost."

"Lost doesn't mean it's a fake, does it?" He helped her screw *Seven* back into its frame. "Let's stop for a bite on the way home."

"Give me a second. I need to fix my face."

Lily returned to her office and dialed again. Paul's cell went to voicemail. "Call me—" she began.

"What's taking you so long?" Nick said.

She shoved the phone in her pack and rummaged for her cosmetics bag. "Just looking for my lipstick." Mascara, lipstick, the compact... The swirling galaxy and crystal stars, her mom's legacy, was gone. She fought panic. Where did she see it last? The ladies' room at the airport?

"Something wrong?" Nick said.

Paul's bathroom at the Ritz. If a maid found it, would she turn it in? Suddenly she had to be alone. She'd try Paul again in the morning. And talk to Michel.

"Lily?"

"Drop me at my condo?"

"You sure?"

"Just drive me home!"

"Yes ma'am." He saluted like a good little scout. "Friday can't come soon enough."

Chapter Thirty-Two

Paul watched the museum's loading dock. It was 8:00 p.m. on Thursday, and for the past three days he'd been surveilling Nick Lang.

Nick lived in an historic neighborhood by Cheesman Park. Its residents were a mixed bag of yuppies who could afford to fix up century-old Denver Squares like Nick's, unrepentant throwbacks to the hippie era who lived off their 401(k)s, and transients who rented by the month in a three-story apartment building cater-corner to his house.

He was a boring surveillance subject. Or played a boring game.

At 7:00 a.m. Nick ventured out in a ratty robe, fetched his *Post*, and waved to the retired guy who drank coffee on his porch across the street. Then he sat at what appeared to be a computer in his enclosed front porch. Around noon he emerged again to water a scraggly rosebush and his doggy patch of grass. Except for those events, and trips to Sprouts and the cleaner's, he spent his days inside and his nights alone—when he wasn't with her. This evening he'd departed from his routine. Paul had tailed Nick to the museum and watched him enter at the loading ramp. Now he was waiting for him to emerge. After hours the loading dock, manned by Ops, was the museum's only exit.

Except for catnaps when he was sure Nick was in for the night, Paul hadn't slept since Tuesday. He'd showered and changed his clothes once, and the floor of his rental car was littered with taco wrappers and Starbucks cups. Though the

FBI's Art Theft Team spent more time on computers than in stakeouts, and it was ages since he'd functioned on caffeine and adrenaline, he liked being in the field. But this case had gone sideways from day one.

Paul glanced at his phone. A couple of calls from Lily, which she'd apparently thought the better of, and three more messages from Susan Grace. As he'd done all week, he ignored them.

There they are.

He watched Nick escort Lily down the ramp. Holding hands, the lovebirds circled the pedestrian plaza to the parking garage. When Nick's vehicle emerged and turned onto the street, Paul was two car lengths behind. He followed them to her condo. He steeled himself for Nick accompanying her in. After a mercifully brief embrace, she went in alone. Would Nick park at his place and return? But Nick headed back through Cheesman Park towards downtown. After tailing him for five minutes, Paul turned around.

Now or never.

He parked down the street from Nick's. He checked his gym bag for his flashlight and tools. Nick's neighbors had no dogs or security cameras and the house next door was vacant, with a *For Sale* sign. He sauntered down the block and into Nick's yard. He was looking for three things: the murder weapon, how Nick got Kurtz to let him into his house, and how he gassed him.

Nick's alarm system was strictly Home Depot, not what you'd expect from a hotshot engineer. Paul put on his gloves. He easily disabled the alarm, then broke a window in the side door and unlocked the deadbolt. The door stuck, indicating it was seldom used. A little luck and Nick wouldn't realize he'd been broken into until it was too late. The first floor was four steps up from the side landing, the basement eight steps down. He had to work fast; there was no telling when Nick would return. He started on the second floor.

The spare bedroom had a drafting table, a high-intensity lamp, and trays neatly organized into T-squares, compasses, drafting tools, and dividers. A box of Xacto knives with razor-sharp blades. Not the murder weapon, but Paul photographed them with his cell. The shelves were filled with art books: drawing manuals, treatises on materials and techniques, a tome on the restoration of oil paintings, and a mini-library on Gustave Caillebotte, including his catalogue raisonné in French. It was stuffy upstairs. Despite Nick's artistic pretensions, Nick was too cheap to spring for centralized air conditioning too.

Paul rifled through the bureau in the master bedroom. He moved to the closet. Inside were one halfway decent suit, two midrange jackets, some laundered and pressed dress shirts and slacks, and a filthy pair of tennis shoes. The brass bed was a tangle of sheets. Picking up a pillow, Paul caught a familiar scent. Bright and astringent, a hint of forest pine— *hers.* Under the bed were socks and a torn condom wrapper. In the master bath he saw a brush with fine blonde hairs.

Get a grip. She's not why you're here.

If the rest of Nick's house was this clean, he was risking his career for nothing. He looked around in frustration. The best place to hide something was in plain sight.... Who stored dirty sneakers in an upstairs closet? Tucked into the toe of one was a thumb drive. He brought it downstairs to Nick's computer. Like the alarm, surprisingly dinky for an engineer. Where did he keep his real computer, the good stuff? The drive was slow to boot up. When it did, the tease abruptly ended.

The first image was of her naked on her side in the brass bed, facing away from the camera. Did Lily know she was being filmed? The camera was set on a timer. The next shots showed her waking up, stretching, opening her arms and displaying her breasts to an invisible lover. Nick entered the frame. There were angry red scratch marks on his back. Was the camera in the ceiling? Him mounting her, thrusting... Fast-forwarding was like flipping through a deck of porn cards. Paul turned the computer off. The screen went blank, but Nick was still astride her, pulsing in Paul's cortex like a bucking bronco in the neon sign of a bar on Colfax.

Nail him for Kurtz.

Paul ejected the thumb drive and put it in his pocket. He made quick work of the living room, dining room and kitchen. The clock over the stove said 9:10. He'd spent more time at Nick's computer than he realized. Was the basement worth a look? If Nick surprised him...

He opened the refrigerator.

Takeout containers, moldy bologna, and five forty-ounce tallboys. The cans were unlabeled. He reached for one. It was a bit unwieldy, heavier than he'd expected. The walls didn't have quite the same give as a twelve-ounce can. Was there liquid inside? He gave it a little shake to see if it sloshed. It didn't. He pulled the tab. Beer shot up and foamed onto the linoleum floor.

Shit.

He mopped up with paper towels. Nick was just squirrelly enough to brew his own beer. On hands and knees, Paul paused.

Kurtz had a weakness for beer.

He thought back to his undergraduate chemistry classes—equilibrium and gas. If you sealed methane in a can, how much pressure would it take for it to explode? It didn't have to be big, just enough to send gas into Kurtz's mouth or up his nose. Hell, Nick didn't even need gas. He could fill that can with liquid methane, or raw sewage, and spritz in some carbon dioxide to stir things up. A tallboy was even better because the narrowness of the can would increase the pressure. He might have to add something to equalize it or coat the inside with epoxy or a polymer so the can didn't collapse on itself, but anyone smart enough to design a battery to take down the fossil fuel industry was clever enough to pressurize a can.

An exploding can of shit.

What else would Nick need? A syphon, a sealing system... It was 9:25, he could be home any minute. Time to search one more place. Basement, or garage?

Exiting by the side door, Paul spent a precious moment reconnecting the alarm. He snuck through the backyard, hugging the shadow from the garage wall. There were three ways in: the roof, which had solar panels and some sort of vent; a window covered from the inside with oil paper; and padlocked double doors facing the alley. Moonlight lit the roof like a landing strip. Those solar panels—was

Nick running an illegal grow operation? He was drawing a shitload of power and wanted to stay off the municipal grid. The house closest to the garage was vacant. The one across the alley was dark. In the apartment building a couple of lights were on.

Get a warrant.

Nick's house was clean except for the tallboys and thumb drive. Because he'd broken in, nothing he found could be used in court. What he was doing wasn't just futile. It was illegal. But if Nick used beer to lure and gas Kurtz, he had to produce the can somewhere.

Is this asshole worth my career?

Call it a night. Go back to the Ritz, talk to Johnson tomorrow—Nick thrusting into Lily pulsed in his head.

Fuck it.

He snapped the padlock with his bolt-cutters. Inside he turned on his flashlight. Table and work stool. Metal cabinets with diamond-shaped hazmat decals—*Health, Fire, Instability, Specific Hazard*—Paul hadn't seen all four filled in since his days in the Counterterrorism Unit. Whiteboard with formulae, equations, circuit diagrams, a scribbled map. Industrial sink in one corner; in the other, a mini-fridge. On the far wall a glassed-in laminar flow bench with rubber arms and a hood—high-tech, and you had to know enough to use one—and a serious data-processing computer with a big hard drive. That's what was drawing the juice. A small safe anchored in cement—more thumb drives or a triggering device inside? How the hell did Nick fit it all in a two-car garage? Paul looked up.

Not much headroom. His flashlight panned to a drop ceiling. He pushed up on one of the panels. A whole bunch of filters.

Oh, shit.

Chapter Thirty-Three

He needed to recharge. He gassed up and took I-25 north. He rolled down his window to let in the breeze. He hated air conditioning, was at home with the smell of plowed fields and manure. The city lights became flickers in his rearview mirror. He began to relax. He knew every twist and turn of this road, every rough patch of asphalt. He drove northeast on I-76 past Keenesburg and Wiggins. At Fort Morgan he turned onto a rural road. Another mile and he was there. He parked and gazed at where it all began.

Moonlight glinted off the towering silos and elevated ramps of the Western Sugar Cooperative, last of the great beet-processing plants on the Eastern Plains. A vast ghostly field stretched before him. The ramshackle house and tin shed were gone, but the stench of ripe sugar beets filled his head. Sweeter and more putrid than rotting flesh, it clung to his clothes and permeated his skin.

With it came the image of his old man in filthy overalls and sweat-stained hat, rubber boots smeared with sticky pulp, hickory-handled beet topper at his side. How many times did he threaten him with that machete? He remembered the day he brought home his sketch of Junie. Now he thought of Brendan, that gap-toothed, skinny little shit in junior high. Brendan was the teacher's pet; he'd labored for months over his pencil drawing of a John Deere tractor. The art teacher sent it and Junie's portrait to the county fair, but the tractor drew the *oohs* and *aahs*. How could a damn tractor compare to Junie? The night before the judging, he snuck into the tent and spilled ink on Brendan's drawing. They both knew what happened, but Brendan had the sense to keep his mouth shut and Junie took the prize. Brendan stopped drawing after that, and a year later his family lost their farm and moved away. What became of him?

But the image of his old man was seared in his brain. When he showed him Junie's portrait, blue ribbon and all, he squinted drunkenly and laughed. *Think a girl like that's interested in a sissy like you? Why, you're no more a man than...* He stomped on the portrait, shredding it with his stained boots. Like the man with the top hat on Caillebotte's bridge, at that moment it was decided.

He was good at being patient, and it took four years to bait and set the trap. By then, Junie had dropped out of school but he'd kept her alive in his old man's head. Each time he brought home porn, every night while he was drunk. *Think she's as pretty as Junie, Pop? She still lives in Kersey, give her a call.* The day he graduated high school, he sprung the trap. *Guess who's in the shed, Pop. Wanna watch?* His old man beat him to it. He kicked open the door and stepped right into the steel jaws of the leghold trap. He left him locked in that shed, howling like an animal, blood dripping through the teeth sunk clear through his rubber boot.

Who's the expert now, Pop?

In the tin shed's searing heat, without water or food, it took three days for gangrene to set in. The rotting leg smelled like beet pulp but dying was too good. When it was time, he threw him in the bed of the pickup and drove him to Fort Morgan. The fear in his old man's eyes said he'd never tell. They took off his leg below the knee, and when he left the hospital he had nowhere to go. The house and shed were burned to the ground and his son was off to college. He'd kept the leg trap, and the thrill of standing at the precipice: knowing his father's fate was in *his* hands and *he* determined when, where and how.

It was past midnight. Speeding down the dark highway, he savored what led up to his showdown with Kurtz. After Kurtz insulted him, he'd studied Caillebotte's sketchbook and the six *Gennevilliers Plain* landscapes until he could reproduce them in his sleep. Those fields reeked of sewage from the Seine, not Fort Morgan beet pulp, but that was a private joke between him and the Master. Adding the man with the brimmed hat was the obvious answer to Caillebotte's frustration with his landscapes. He knew him so well by then that he was sure that it was what Caillebotte himself would have painted. Why, he even lined the canvas to make it look old!

When he was done, he fed Sully an anonymous tip. *A lost Caillebotte's coming on the market from a private source, and a competing collector's hot to acquire it.* Playing straw man and communicating in writing raised the stakes and the reward. Just as he'd planned, in his grandiosity Kurtz fantasized the man with the hat was Caillebotte, beckoning him to join him in the trees. When Kurtz bought *Seven* and donated it to the museum, he was overjoyed. He didn't just fool Kurtz. His masterpiece had come home.

At first it was a thrill to see *Seven* hanging in the European & American gallery. And all those mousepads and coffee mugs! But then a new yearning set in. What good was it to paint a masterpiece if no one knew you were the artist? And Kurtz's cock-of-the-walk talk, his bragging about rescuing *Seven* from obscurity, began to grate. You'd have thought *he* painted *Seven* himself. But forging a painting was a gift that kept giving, and it was time to take Kurtz down another peg. A homebrew was his entrée.

"I have something to tell you, George."

Kurtz sat in his armchair, in that library with the gold-leafed silk walls, drinking greedily from the tallboy. Jay was right. He wasn't just a hypocrite, he was a pig.

"Oh? And what might that be?"

"Your Caillebotte's a fake."

Kurtz's lips gleamed wetly. "You think I was fooled? Or give a shit?"

"*I* painted it!"

"Of course you did!" Kurtz laughed with real pleasure. "I gave it to the museum because it's inferior." He fixed his beady eyes on him and dug his claws into the arms of the upholstered chair. "That painting means nothing to me, and you're no more an artist than..."

But he and Caillebotte would have the last word.

Now he careened down I-25, nails digging into his steering wheel. The bright lights said he was approaching Denver. On impulse, he continued past his exit to the next one south. Dimming his headlights, he turned down Harry Sparks's block. He pulled to the curb at the red-roofed bungalow and let his engine idle. Through the front window he saw a light go on in the back of the house, the kitchen. Backlit, a small figure crept to the dining room and sat at the table, like his old man in the middle of the night with a bottle of booze. Harry rose, and something flickered at the window. Was he looking at the street, did he see him? Harry limped back to the kitchen and a moment later the light went out. He imagined that heavy tread, left leg dragging ever so slightly, as Harry made his way down the hall and sank into bed.

But this was no time for pity. He was just like his old man and Kurtz.

And Lily was the real threat.

Destroying the Degas hadn't stopped her. Forcing his hand, was she? He was more than up for what came next—*primed,* you might say. If all else failed, the end game was in place. Now he was ready. Tomorrow was the big day. Like the little man with the hat, he knew what bright and shiny bauble would draw her to her fate.

Chapter Thirty-Four

"Here's your affidavit." Paul flung it on Johnson's desk. It was Friday morning and he still hadn't slept.

"For what?"

"To search Nick Lang's house and garage."

Johnson picked up the affidavit and started skimming. "There's an awful lot of 'on information and belief,' Paul. On whose information and belief might that be?"

"Confidential sources."

"Xacto knives, beer cans, brewing equipment ... How's that connected to Kurtz's murder?"

"Lang gassed him with a beer can filled with shit." He'd left the condoms and porn out of the affidavit. "Keep reading."

Johnson snorted. "Laminar flow bench—what the fuck is that?"

"It has rubber sleeves and a hood. It filters air and blows it towards the user. You'll need a hazmat team."

"Towards the user—they teach that crap at Quantico?" He read on. "Metal canisters, suspected chemicals... A safe sunk in concrete?"

"He didn't want anyone walking off with it."

"These items are awfully specific, Paul."

"Affidavits require specificity."

"Sounds like your informant was inside Mr. Lang's house and garage. Is he a burglar, or just a friend?"

"If I told you that, he wouldn't be confidential."

Johnson poured himself another cup of coffee. Probably

still trying to wrap his head around a filtration system that blew contaminants at the user. Not that Paul blamed him.

"Another rough night?" Johnson said.

When I was young, I was just like you. Full of piss and vinegar, ready to kick down doors and pay later, especially if there was a dame...

"This isn't the time to discuss my sex life."

"Or lack thereof," Johnson said. "Son, you know what happens to cops who present false affidavits?"

If the Denver dicks had been doing their job he wouldn't have to. "I'm aware of my professional responsibilities."

"And the penalties for perjury?"

"Those too."

Johnson sighed. "What exactly do you expect me to do with this?"

"Get it to a judge ASAP so he can issue a warrant."

"It's Friday, Paul. I don't know who I can find."

He hung onto his temper. "Do Denver judges take three-day weekends?"

"No, and they're no stupider than the ones in D.C." Johnson waited, apparently for it to sink in. "Take a couple days and think this through. If it really is Nick Lang—"

"We need to get in fast."

Johnson reread the affidavit. "I'll make a few calls. But if we get a judge to sign off—"

"I'm going in with you."

Chapter Thirty-Five

Late that afternoon the warrant was issued. Johnson ignored the advice about the hazmat team but cordoned off Nick's block. With a shower and a fresh suit, Paul felt in command of himself for the first time in days. He'd even bullied Johnson into letting him serve the warrant. Straightening his tie, he walked up to Nick's door with two uniformed cops and rang the bell.

Nick answered barefoot, in jeans. His eyes widened in a show of surprise. "I know you. You're Lily's ex."

Paul handed him the warrant.

Nick ignored it. "Looking for her?"

"Read the warrant."

"Because if it's Lily you want, you're ten years too late."

Paul smiled tightly. "You can wait outside if you like."

Nick opened the door wide. "At your service, officers."

Johnson and his men followed them in. With Nick hovering, they systematically searched his house. In the master bedroom, Nick drew Paul aside. "Did you find the others?"

"What others?"

"That wasn't even the best sex we had," Nick said. Johnson was watching. Paul stepped between him and Nick to block his view. "The thumb drive's not in the warrant. I could file to get it back."

"You're good at filing lawsuits, aren't you? I read your screed against Kurtz."

"Those photos are private. They belong to Lily and me—"

Paul grabbed him by the throat. "You sick fuck. Go near her again, and I'll show them to her."

Nick laughed. "Think she minded?"

A meaty hand gripped Paul's shoulder. "You're needed out front," Johnson said, his expression leaving no room for argument. "We'll come get you when we search the garage."

———

Johnson's men pried open the garage doors. There was no sign of the busted padlock.

"I'll help if you tell me what you're looking for," Nick said as one cop opened a cabinet and another photographed the whiteboard. Nobody wanted to touch the laminar flow bench. "Because frankly, this is a waste of time. George Kurtz meant nothing to me."

"Check the drain and trap," Paul told the cop poking around the sink, "and use gloves." The cop gave him a sour look but pulled on his gloves.

"I didn't kill Kurtz." Nick sounded nervous. "Much as he deserved it."

A detective finally approached the bench. Gingerly he parted the plastic curtain.

"Don't touch that!" Nick cried.

"What the hell is it?" Johnson said.

"A prototype for a long-life battery." He was proud of it, arrogant. "Unlike Tesla's or Samsung's, mine won't catch fire or explode."

Paul snorted. "You'll do anything to protect your inventions, won't you?"

"I just want what's mine."

So do I. "Enough to kill Kurtz?"

"Just destroy his industry. But I'll give you one thing: you really turn her on. After she saw you at the Samurai exhibit, it was the best sex I ever had. Next time I'll add audio...."

Don't do it.

"...the way she moaned, I'd say it was the best sex she—"

He hit Nick as hard as he could in the face. Something broke.

"What the—" Johnson grabbed his arm.

Eye socket, nose? Too much blood to tell.

Through the red, Nick grinned. "This isn't over."

———

"I can't believe you thought a lithium ion battery was a bomb," Johnson said.

"Don't rub it in."

They were in a cop dive drinking whisky and chasers. Paul no longer had to worry about Susan Grace. The last time he looked at his cell, there was a message from the FBI Director.

"Nick ain't our guy, Paul."

"Yeah, I know. He's an engineer and a home-brewer, not a fucking maniac."

"If you don't give a shit about your own career, you could've at least given a moment's thought to the reputation of the Denver Police Department."

"I'm sorry."

But Johnson was more amused than pissed. "A wise man knows the difference between what he wants and what he needs, Paul...."

What difference does it make? I've lost both.

"...lucky if Lang doesn't sue you for everything you've got."

"He won't."

"Why?"

"I have something of his."

Johnson knew better than to ask. "My boys will keep their mouths shut, but you're damn lucky he isn't the killer."

"I know."

"Cheer up." Johnson threw him a friendly punch. "Maybe she'll be impressed."

"With what?"

"You've got quite a left hook. Some gals like that."

"She's not the type." At least she was safe. Nick wouldn't go near her now, and if he wasn't the killer, it wasn't anyone else in her orbit.

"I have yet to meet a woman—" Johnson began.

"Spare me."

Johnson ordered another round. "Have you considered talking to her?"

"About what?"

"Oh, I don't know. Why you've been making such an ass of yourself for the past two months? I'm sure it hasn't escaped her attention."

Paul tossed back his drink. "Too late for that."

And where would I even start?

Chapter Thirty-Six

When Lily badged in before the museum opened on Friday, Ops had already rehung *Seven*. She phoned Paul again and got no answer. She called Michel. His executive assistant said he was out until Monday.

"This is urgent, Joan." *The centerpiece of his collection is a fake.* "Can he be reached?"

"I'm afraid not." Joan's voice softened. "If it's about your resignation, we all feel just terrible—"

"It's about a painting."

"Michel said only if it's a family emergency."

"It is." *Aren't we all just one big happy—*

Joan's professionalism was firmly in place. "He told me to expect your resignation today. Can Gina help?"

Lily gritted her teeth. Until she reached Paul, the least she could do was get the goddamned painting taken down. With her colleagues starting to trickle in, she dialed Gina.

"We have to take *Seven* down, Gina. It's a fake."

Gina laughed. "I'm not surprised. Leave it to you to try to depart this institution by claiming a masterpiece was forged. Could you possibly go any lower?"

Payback for the other night with Paul? "This has nothing to do with my job. I have proof—"

"You only get one Schiele."

"At least tell Paul!"

Gina hung up.

Until he surfaced, there was nothing she could do. Lily angrily typed a one-line resignation and cleaned out her desk. The Objects Conservator and her assistant were at a symposium in Cleveland. Amy stayed in her cubicle. To Lily's relief, at mid-morning Amy and the rest of the staff left for a Conservation Committee meeting.

When her desk was clear, she started on her bookshelves. Binders of memoranda, tomes on painting technique, a chemistry treatise from grad school. She agonized over what to do with her snake plant. Its sword-like leaves thrived on neglect. She left it on Amy's desk.

What will I do for a job?

She called Sean, but he, too was gone for the weekend.

As the clock ticked down on Lily's final day at the museum, her anger and frustration grew. She was no closer to identifying Kurtz's killer. What would Sean do? Go for the chemistry, the trace elements on Kurtz's body. Did the killer wipe him down before he stabbed him? She pulled up the autopsy report on her computer.

Kurtz was clothed when he was killed. The blade penetrated his shirt and left fibers and chemicals in the wounds. That meant the chemicals were on the knife. She scrolled through the crime scene photos. *What's hiding in plain sight?* She tried forwarding them to her home computer, but they were encrypted. Until Paul surfaced, she was at the end of the road. She deleted the files and turned to her final status reports. At 6:05 p.m. she checked her e-mail one last time. There was an urgent plea from the Objects Conservator, with a photo of an ornate melon-shaped samurai helmet attached. Boys loved armor and weapons; apparently one young visitor couldn't resist touching it. Docents and gallery hosts were required to report those events, and a conservator had to ensure the lacquer was intact.

Until I send Michel my resignation, I'm still a goddamned conservator.

She e-mailed her colleague back. But the gallery was now closed.

Her key card gave her master access to exhibition halls. Blockbusters like the Van Gogh had guards stationed inside at night, but smaller exhibitions like the Samurai were monitored by 24/7 cameras and Israeli alarms that detected movement. After hours, the galleries were secured by wire with bicycle locks. She called Frank.

"I need to inspect a helmet in Samurai."

She left her backpack on her desk and locked the lab. She crossed the bridge to the main exhibition gallery. A newer member of the security staff, brawny young Joey, met her there. He had a dab of red sauce on his chin.

"Want me to stay, Ms. Sparks?"

"Finish your dinner, Joey. I'll call when I'm done."

He switched on the lights and locked the gallery behind her.

Lily made her way past the Samurai in full regalia to the three warhorses. A mural of warriors fanning their troops into battle extended to the room behind them, to unify the display and distract visitors from having to circle around the partition. The helmet in question belonged to one of the group of Samurai standing at eye level behind the velvet rope on the other side. She could have squeezed through the opening between the horses' platform and the next room, but out of respect for the exhibition's designer took the long way around.

She remembered this particular group of Samurai from opening night. Her warrior was to the right, next to the partition. His chain mail and plated armor required a balancing act; his hips and arms bent forward and his upper body leaned back. His helmet was the most spectacular: melon-shaped, with a gold chrysanthemum at its crown and wings extending from the sides. His throat guard had a leather strap and a hole to release sweat. His grimace was more outraged than fierce.

"You poor dear."

In the bright light his expression seemed comical. His eyebrows arched as if they shared a private joke.

She glanced at the photo on her cell and began examining the helmet. Its visor and iron plates were inlaid with silver vines and delicate leaves. The inlay looked intact. She stepped back for a longer view. A faint rustle came from the vicinity of the Samurai at the forefront. In the corner of her eye, something flickered. She looked again.

Nothing.

A trick of light on his helmet, compounded by the

busyness of the mural on the wall. That was it. Or maybe it glinted off his short sword. He was the only one with a weapon. She glanced sideways at the adjacent display. Was some of the armor missing, along with a sword? The one they used to disembowel themselves. A wakizashi. The Objects Conservator must have taken the armor and sword down. Taking another step back, she scrutinized the Samurai again.

There were five. She remembered four.

They fanned out behind their leader like a pack of dogs.

Suddenly the gallery went black. The darkness was as soft and dense as a blindfold.

Did Ops forget she was there? With the display at the center of the maze, she couldn't see the *Exit* sign. She visualized the layout. Partition to her right, five paces behind her a case of masks. Past the masks, the path curved back to the warhorses. From them it was more or less a straight shot to the door. No reason to panic. A flute softly began to play, accompanied by singing like a banshee's wail.

"Joey?"

She took three deep breaths to clear her head. She was there to document the condition of that helmet. Raising her cell phone, she took another step back and focused on where the melon-shaped headgear should be. Her camera flashed just as the Samurai with the wakizashi moved. She blinked to refocus. He was at the rope. He lifted his leg to climb over it.

Oh, shit.

As it brushed against chain mail, the wakizashi clanked. She saw Kurtz riven from his pelvis up, gutted and his entrails smeared on the wall. The Samurai clambered over the rope.

This isn't a joke. He's going to kill me!

But she was paralyzed, frozen. In a black lake, trapped under a glazed crust with an immense hand dragging her away from the bank. The monster in the lake was back. Her chest burned from holding her breath. Her head was about to explode—*don't breathe!* She took a massive gulp. *No...* But instead of icy water flooding her, it was a whisper of something foul. She was in the Samurai Exhibition. This monster was real.

Swish. Air brushed her cheek as he drew his wakizashi

back.

Get to those horses.

She leaped forward and to the right. Her shoulder hit the partition, but she squeezed through the crack. Behind her came the crash of armor.

Blindly, she felt her way to the horses. Another crash— did he hit a display case? She dove under the stallion in the center. Grabbing hold of his stirrups, she hoisted herself up. She barely reached around his girth, but she was light enough and had the leverage to cling to the stirrups and his belly. Her arms throbbed. She tucked her knees to her chest. How long could she hold on?

He was in front of the horses now. His breath was fetid. The air swished as he moved to the stallion to her right. Chain mail clinked as it hit a stirrup. He had a heavy, shambling gait... Her shoulders and legs burned. He grunted in frustration. In one moment—

Brrrinnggg!

Her cell.

The Samurai turned.

She closed her eyes and prayed.

Chapter Thirty-Seven

"Ms. Sparks?" A blinding light shone in her eyes.

"Joey?"

He helped her down from the horse, taking her weight as she let go of one stirrup and then the other. Her arms were frozen, elbows locked and fingers spasming. Then she was shaking so badly she couldn't stand. Joey sat her on the platform. He spoke into his walkie-talkie. The gallery lights came on and he turned off his flashlight. Did he frighten the Samurai away?

"You saw him?" she said.

"Who?" Joey's brown eyes showed concern.

"The Samurai. The one with the sword."

"In the display?"

"No! He's real, not a mannequin." She made herself slow down. "I had to do an object report."

"On the horse?"

"No, a helmet. The lights went out—"

"They were on when I left you."

Did he think *she* turned them off? "Then the music started to play."

"Music?" None now.

"He came out of that group of Samurai behind the partition, Joey. There were five of them, not four. He had a wakizashi."

Joey looked at her doubtfully. With the lights on and him beside her, she began to feel foolish. But his gallantry prevailed. "Let's take a look."

They took the normal route from the horses to the group of Samurai. Four warriors stood on the platform. The one with the wakizashi was gone.

"I took a photo. Maybe I caught him." Trembling, she pulled out her cell. The caller had been her dad, who never left messages. The photo was a blur. But even with the lights out, the security cameras in the ceiling detected movement. "Did your monitor get a signal?"

"If it did, it was probably you. Let's badge you out."

Now she understood. Ops knew she was fired. They didn't even trust her to badge herself out. She shook her head. "My backpack's in the lab."

"I'll escort you." She was being eighty-sixed from a bar.

Joey waited while she gathered her things. He was too polite to comment on the cartons and bare shelves. The thought of being escorted from the building—surrendering her lanyard and badge at the loading dock like a common thief—was suddenly unbearable.

Until I send Michel my resignation, I am the fucking Conservator of Paintings.

"I'll be down in a minute," she said. "I have to write that report."

"Frank told me to wait."

"No!" Her vehemence surprised her. "I'll see you downstairs."

Joey hesitated. "If there's anything—"

"Tell Frank I'll be down in five minutes to badge myself out."

———

When Joey left, she sank into her chair. Now she was angry.

How could they not believe her?

That Samurai was real. He knew the museum well enough to gain entrance to a gallery, hide there after it closed, and exit without being seen. He rigged some kind of remote to control the lights. He armed and armored himself from the adjacent display. Did he work at the museum, or was he just ballsy enough to steal an access card?

It was past 7:00 p.m. In the building across the park,

people were working late or having an office party. Did he come after her because of Kurtz? And where was he now? In her lab she was safe. Ops knew she was there and she'd said five minutes. She had to pull herself together.

She turned on her desk lamp and got out her makeup bag. Where was her compact? She searched for it, then remembered it was gone. God, how she missed it! She shakily applied her lip gloss blind, then speed-dialed her dad but got no answer. Booting up her computer for the last time, she wrote and filed the incident report. *Work inspected, no damage noted.* With a defiant flick of her finger, she sent her resignation to Michel. The silence was broken by the familiar rumble of the freight elevator creaking up the shaft.

Workmen made deliveries at night. The museum was bigger than her, a universe that would continue after she was gone. The elevator shuddered to a halt. The doors opened with a groan. The delivery man would be surprised—

"Hello?" she said. She rose and went to her doorway. Like the galleries, the lab was windowless. The only light came from the elevator. *Clinkety-clank.* The doors closed, plunging the lab into darkness. But someone was there.

"Amy?" she said.

Whoomph. The elephant trunk over the heat vacuum table blasted on. It did that throughout the day to vent solvents, but at night? Under the noise she sensed a coiled energy.

Ops knows I'm here.

"Joey?"

She looked at the heat vacuum table. The illuminated readout said the heat on both sides was on. Solvents and varnishes were flammable. Leaving the table on was worse than careless. She reached to shut it off.

"Nick?"

A blast of dry heat hit her.

A strange odor—chemical or electrical—came from the table. It was on full blast. She reached again for the controls. The floor trembled. Someone was behind her. She froze.

This isn't happening again.

His tread was slow and deliberate, smoother without the armor. He smelled of oil and metal and sweat. He circled the table like a wolf corralling its prey.

He came back to finish the job.

She made her legs move. With each of his steps, she took one back. He wasn't a monster and this wasn't a lake. Ops knew she was here and—

He's human. This is my turf.

She knew every weapon in the lab. Paintbrushes in the top drawer of the cabinet by the broom closet. A ferrule—the crimped metal band that kept the bristles in place—could take out an eye. Syringes in the second drawer—harder to aim. Tacking iron on the counter—heats to 425 degrees, metal nose tapered to get in tight. Scalpels, medical grade, in the drawer directly behind her... She grabbed one. It was cool and sharp.

The lamp on the wheeled stand lit like a phosphorous bomb.

Tilted in her face, its twin black filaments pulsed like eyes in a demented moon. Blinded, she flailed, but it was like swinging a broomstick at a moving piñata under a strobe. Her head hit something hard—a vacuum hood. She was trapped between the table and the spray bath. His breath on her cheek was a foul kiss.

She aimed high and thrust as hard as she could. Her scalpel cut through meat to bone. A grunt of surprise, a howl of rage. Before she could do it again, he lunged. She threw out her left arm. She hit the table.

A second scream, higher pitched, filled the lab. A smell like burned meat.

He stumbled towards the broom closet. The door creaked and caught. Something heavy fell. Scrabbling, metal against metal as the rusted door to the roof was wrenched open. That terrible scream—like an animal in a trap—again and again.

Is that me?

Chapter Thirty-Eight

Pounding at the main door.

Is he back?

Gripping the scalpel, she crouched behind the table. That awful smell…

"Ms. Sparks?" A kind voice, concerned.

The overhead lights went on.

"Jesus!" Frank kneeled beside her. He took the scalpel away. He and Joey looked scared. "Your hand's bleeding. And good lord, your arm …."

"He threw me on the table." The words sounded like they came from someone else. "He—"

"Who?" Frank looked at Joey. "We need to get her downstairs." He put his arm around her shoulders. He lifted her to her feet. She squeezed her eyes against the light and started to shake. "Are you cold?"

She began to cry.

"Ms. Sparks—"

"He used the freight elevator."

Frank turned to Joey. "Was the elevator here when you left?"

"No, I—"

Her right hand throbbed. She couldn't feel her left arm. Frank's expression said it was bad. "He went out by the roof."

Joey went to the broom closet. "The door to the roof's open."

Now they'll believe me.

But her attacker was gone.

—

In the Ops office, Frank swabbed her hand with antiseptic. He wrapped it tightly in gauze. Gently he turned over her left arm.

"Jeez!" Joey said.

From elbow to wrist, most of the skin was gone. What was left looked strange. Bubbly.

Frank turned to Joey. "Call 911."

"Just give me a couple Advil." She started to rise. "Denver Health's on my way home."

Frank stared. He spoke slowly, like an adult to a child. "Lily, I don't think you understand. You'll lose the use of your arm if it gets infected."

She sat and let him wrap her arm loosely. He gave her two Tylenol with codeine from his private stash. Suddenly cold, she reached for her hoodie. He draped it over her shoulder.

"I'm filing a police report," she said.

"On the burglar in the lab?" Frank said.

"He wasn't a burglar." Now she was almost too warm. Was it the codeine? "He attacked me in the Samurai exhibit and came back to finish the job."

The men exchanged a glance. "We'll do that Monday."

Frank doesn't believe me either.

"The man who attacked me works at the museum."

"Let Joey drive you to the ER."

Three blocks from her condo was a walk-in clinic. She'd go first thing tomorrow—if she made it out of here alive. The codeine was definitely kicking in. She rubbed her eyes. Her face felt foreign, and the pain in her hand made it hard to focus. She painted on a smile for Frank.

"Straight to Denver Health. Cross my heart and hope to die."

Chapter Thirty-Nine

Friday night crowds were heading for the bars, and LoDo's unending construction funneled traffic into two lanes. The Prius inched down Speer Boulevard. Her hand throbbed. Hospital, or the police? This wasn't over. Far from it.

He must have stolen a museum ID. She'd never thought twice about leaving her backpack in the lab. If he took her ID and copied it, he could have her new condo key too. Stalled at a light, she pulled out her phone. The codeine put her in the worst of all worlds: fuzzy and in pain. Her arm felt like it didn't belong to her. Her shoulders and chest ached from clinging to the horse. It was unreal. Maybe Nick had something stronger than codeine. She speed-dialed him and got no answer. She passed Denver Health and was stopped by traffic. Scrolling for messages, she saw her dad had called again. Kurtz, the Degas, Jack... Who would the killer go after now, when he couldn't get her?

Dad.

Cutting off an SUV, she got into the turn lane. With this traffic the bungalow was twenty minutes away. Would the killer beat her there? Ignoring furious honks, she wove in and out of cars on University Boulevard. Her hand made it hard to grip the wheel.

A siren blared.

What the hell?

Before she could pull over, a firetruck roared up behind her. Like a train barreling through a crossing, a red blur zoomed past. A second truck followed.

She drove on. The sky lightened to yellow and pink. A false dawn. The closer she drew to his house the brighter it was. His street was closed off. She smelled smoke. On the next block she screeched to the curb.

"Stop, miss…"

She shook off the cop's hand and ran to the bungalow. The McMansion at the corner was untouched, but her dad's roof was on fire. His windows stared like a blind man's eyes. Behind them something flickered and burned.

Firemen herded neighbors in nightclothes to safety across the street. *Gas,* she heard a fireman say. She grabbed his arm.

"My dad's in there!"

He nodded, then huddled with his partners. A third truck and ambulance arrived. She watched them unroll a flat canvas hose. They shrugged on heavy vests as methodically as surgeons scrubbing up. But surgeons failed too. Three firemen marched up the walk. The flames were at the front door. Suddenly the walls buckled and swelled.

The bungalow exploded.

Debris flew like pickup sticks, sending the crowd back.

The house burned like a candle, flaming blue at the center and blossoming into red-orange petals with yellow tips. Someone said *Aaaah…*

She saw something on the lawn.

"Dad!"

He was black with smoke and in his underwear. A fireman ran to him. Others followed. They waved frantically for a medic. Two EMTs rushed over. They laid him on a gurney and clamped an oxygen mask over his mouth.

"He's my dad!" His hair and eyebrows were singed. His eyes didn't focus. They lifted the gurney into the back of the ambulance. He gagged.

"Good sign," an EMT said over his shoulder. "How old is he?"

"Seventy-six." *Next year, please let him make it….*

One EMT set up an IV drip. Another slapped inside his elbow for a vein. When the bag was connected they heaved sighs of relief. They covered him with a warming blanket. She climbed in back and took his hand. Did she imagine him squeezing back?

"We're taking him to Swedish," the driver said.

She wiped his face. Under the soot he was grey. He looked very young and very old. The blanket made him a child-sized bag of bones. *Nine lives, Dad,* she whispered, *like Jack.*

He opened his eyes and winked.

An EMT frowned. "Miss, you really shouldn't—"

"I'm coming."

Chapter Forty

Men in scrubs rushed him to the ER. She gave a nurse his information. The door swung open. Doctors bent over him.

"Can I see him?"

"Not yet."

The waiting room had a bored cop and a woman with a broken nose. Lily sat near the swinging doors. The cop finished his coffee and sauntered down the hall. The woman left with a man who might have been her husband. A closed-circuit TV played videos about the importance of flu shots and the role of diet in treating diabetes. The codeine had definitely worn off. Finally an older doctor in scrubs emerged and spoke to the nurse.

Lily went to the counter.

"You're his daughter?" The doc had wire-rimmed glasses and a neat beard. He motioned her to follow him into the ER. The activity centered on her dad in a bay with open curtains. "We stabilized him."

"Is he conscious?"

"More or less. We're waiting for test results before moving him to the ICU."

"But he's okay?"

"Mainly smoke inhalation. He's dehydrated and on an IV, but he's a tough old bird."

Her eyes welled. So much she wanted to tell him, things she'd never said. "Can I speak to him?"

"For a minute." The doctor was looking at the gauze on her hand. "Is that something—"

She shook her head. "I need to see my dad."

He was hooked up to oxygen and wasn't so grey. The IV port was in the back of one hand. She lifted the other and kissed it. It was wiry but fragile, with age spots. He couldn't stand to be idle or cooped up inside. Amazing how alike they were.

"Dad?"

His eyes flew open. Recognizing her, he tried to give a thumb's-up.

"Lie still," she said.

He tugged at his mask. A nurse started to readjust it, but he shook his head. His fingers gripped hers. "My house..."

"Gone, Dad."

His eyes widened with panic.

She patted his hand. "You can come home with me later. Lounge on the balcony and watch ballgames with Jack." He relaxed his grip. The nurse reconnected his oxygen mask.

An orderly gave the doctor a sheaf of X-rays and printouts and wheeled him to the ICU.

"Test results?" she asked. But the doctor was looking at her again. More specifically, her hand. Before she could jam it in her pocket, he was unwrapping the gauze. The two-inch gash in her palm oozed a colorless fluid. "I cut it."

"With a scalpel?"

"It's fine."

"Let's hope so." He took her by the elbow to an examination room. She gasped. "Your arm?" He signaled for a nurse.

With bandage scissors he cut through Frank's gauze. The flesh on the back of her forearm was raw and red. The blisters were wet and ugly. He touched one with a swab. She blanched.

"Pain is good," he said. "When was your last tetanus shot?" He administered the shot and a systemic antibiotic. The nurse brought a surgical tray. "This will hurt," he warned. "Want a valium?"

"That's all you've got?"

He gave her a Percocet, then injected her hand with liquid fire. Before she could protest, he stitched the wound up. She closed her eyes and surrendered to the drug. More pricks in her forearm. Then it was bathed in something wet and cool. When she opened her eyes, her arm was swaddled like a baby. The skin above and below the bandage was painted golden brown.

"You may need skin grafts," the doctor said. "Too soon to tell."

"How's my dad?"

"You're in worse shape than he is, though he could stand to gain a few pounds." He leaned back in his chair. "What happened tonight?"

"His bungalow exploded."

"That explains your dad, but what about you?"

"A lab accident."

He peered at her curiously. "That's not a chemical burn."

"I'm a conservator at a museum."

"Conservators use scalpels?"

"Occasionally."

He took off his glasses and rubbed his eyes. "I want to admit you overnight." He tried to make a joke of it. "At least you'll be safe."

How long was it since someone believed her? Not Frank, or Joey. Or Paul. "I—" She stopped. Too much to explain. "How about me hanging out tonight at the ICU with him instead?"

"That's a deal." The doctor looked relieved.

"And you're keeping him in the hospital awhile, right?" She couldn't protect him at the condo. She couldn't even protect herself.

"Is there someone—" He thought the better of it. "That sounds like a good idea all around." But something seemed to be bothering him.

"How is he really?" she asked.

The doctor put his glasses back on. He shuffled through the reports again. "Smoke inhalation, as I said. At your dad's age that's not trivial, but..." He held up an X-ray and frowned. Her breath caught. "I'm more concerned about his leg."

She exhaled. "You mean the polio."

"Who said he had polio?"

"He got it as a boy."

"There's no sign of it." The doctor was emphatic. "His leg was fractured, a nasty break."

"From tonight?"

"At least thirty years ago..."

Her head spun.

"...was your dad in a car accident?"

Chapter Forty-One

Lily spent the night in the ICU at his side. In the morning they moved him to a private room. He was off the IV. When he complained about his soft-boiled eggs and the oxygen cannula making his nose itch, she knew it was okay for her to go home. He'd be safe here, and she was relieved not to have to make small talk. The only thing she wanted to talk about was what happened thirty years ago when her mom died.

At the condo she fed Jack. She yearned for a hot shower and settled for a change of clothes. She tried Nick again. No answer. She knocked on Louise's door.

"Can you take Jack for a few days?"

"Of course!" Louise made no effort to conceal her delight. "Are you going on a trip?"

"No. I just—" Kurtz's killer had already tangled with Jack. He had no reason to go after Louise.

"What happened to your arm, dear?"

"A little accident at work. I'm not supposed to lift anything."

"Well, don't you worry about Jack," Louise assured her. "We're good friends."

When this is over, will I even have a cat?

The cops had brushed off the break-ins at her condo. Frank and Joey thought she was crazy. The ER doc had done his part by being generous with the Percocet and checking her dressing before going off duty. To whom could she turn? Paul and Nick were MIA. She certainly couldn't depend on her dad.

What's Kurtz's killer doing right now?

Her scalpel had penetrated meat, she'd heard his anguished moan. Like her, he'd be nursing his wound and gathering strength. Was he in the crowd watching when the bungalow blew? He'd have to move pretty damn fast to rig it to explode so soon after attacking her in the lab. Which meant he'd cut the gas line beforehand. He planned to kill her dad all along. They'd survived. But he'd come after them again.

Her arm hurt. She wanted a Percocet.

Think about the killer.

He forged *Seven* and butchered Kurtz to make a point.

Think, think, think. Her hand thumped like a snare drum in her head. Pain, and anger. At the killer, Paul. Her dad. Was anything he ever said true? He'd lied about the polio. What else was a lie? And how could she confront him now, with the killer out there, and when he'd barely survived his bungalow exploding?

Who will I be if I look away from the truth now?

He'd cultivated her perfect eye. He'd raised her to believe her perceptions were infallible, that all that mattered was what she saw. But she wasn't perfect. She'd been blind to *Seven* and to him. What else had she missed? Paul was right about that too. There was only one thing to do.

Go ask your lying father.

———

The sign on Brandt Gallery of Fine Art's door said *Closed*. Through the window Lily saw Elena and a man with a Van Dyke beard and an elegant sport coat. She knocked on the glass. Elena answered in a zebra-striped caftan and ankle-high velvet boots. Her customer looked put off.

"Hope I'm not interrupting," Lily said.

"You?" Elena smiled. "Never."

Her new exhibition, *The Modern Muse*, was winding down. The massive oils were by late twentieth-century female artists, some of whom had inspired their more famous male peers. The show had drawn excellent reviews and a well-heeled crowd. Almost every painting had a red sticker indicating it was sold. The pièce de resistance was an enormous ochre, crimson and cobalt canvas with a jagged black center. Elena's customer was peering at it intently.

"Geoffrey's one of my best collectors," Elena whispered to Lily. "Vaginas don't frighten him. When he comes back, he'll buy."

She turned back to Geoffrey, who pecked her on the cheek. With a stiff nod in Lily's direction, he left. Elena locked the door behind him. Behind her outsized glasses, her eyes sharpened with concern.

"Are you all right, my dear?"

The paintings, her mentor, the sheer civility of the gallery almost made Lily forget why she'd come. She couldn't put Elena at risk. But to go after Kurtz's killer she had to trust herself again. How fitting to seek help in dealing with her fraud of a father, from the woman who was as close to a mother as she'd ever had.

"A lab accident." *Lie enough times and maybe it'll become true.* Elena's shrewd gaze said she wasn't fooled. "I need your advice."

"About the FBI man?"

"My father."

"Let's sit." Elena had met her dad once and liked him. She gestured to the divan in back. "What happened?"

"He's been lying to me."

Elena laughed. "We do that to protect those we love, Lily."

"He was protecting himself, not me."

"And you think pulling off a scab will make you whole?"

"Not just any scab, Elena. How my mother died."

"Sometimes the greater good is accepting who you are, Lily." She smiled to take the sting out of it. "Sleep on it tonight. Tomorrow's soon enough."

"But I can't just—"

"Is it so bad not to know the truth, if it spoils the illusion?"

Never ask where a painting comes from, or what it costs.

What else did Elena turn a blind eye to, what did she regret? But ignorance was a luxury Lily could no longer afford. She rose and kissed Elena's cheek.

"Don't look too closely, Lily. See too much and it stays with you forever."

———

When Lily arrived at Swedish, her dad was flirting with a young carrot-haired nurse. He scowled comically and the nurse giggled. Seeing her in the doorway, he waved her in like an impresario. All he needed was a top hat and cane.

"Your dad's a real charmer," the nurse said.

"I brought him food." She'd stopped at Boston Market on the way.

"Doc said to fatten him up. Whatever he wants, he can have." The nurse patted his arm and left.

Lily unpacked the sweet corn and mashed potatoes. His eyes lit up at the food.

"That's my girl. I can always count on you, Lily."

She fed him a couple mouthfuls, then gave him the spoon. "The doctor says you'll be fine."

He shrugged. "I don't know what happened. Damn thing blew up."

That bungalow had been all that was left of her past. The Franciscan ware, her old bedroom where he'd tucked her in and read to her, the door where her mom stood that last time. All in smithereens. What did those losses mean to him? He looked so vulnerable in his flannel gown with the heart monitors on his chest. Watching him dig into his potatoes with childlike glee, Lily wondered if she knew him at all.

"How's your leg?"

The spoon stopped halfway to his mouth. "What do you mean?"

Was Elena right, was it better not to know how he truly injured it? She'd never told him about Paul. Wasn't he entitled to secrets of his own? *But he lied.* "The doctor said it never healed."

He smiled ruefully. "Polio's a gift that keeps giving, Lily."

And a father's love, does that keep giving too?

"He says you broke it in an accident."

He set down his spoon. Dusk was falling. The only illumination was the light over his bed. It made his face look naked. For an instant she saw him as a boy, uncertain and pure. He blinked, and his innocence was replaced with the imperious expression she knew so well.

"Remember our walks? What did I teach you, Lily?"

"Nothing matters but what you see." *Who, what, when and where. Never why.*

"Why do you think I taught you that?"

"To protect me." *Because the one time you didn't look, it cost my mom her life?*

"Damn right." He pushed away his tray. "Look at me, Lily. What do you see?"

The father who'd loved her all her life, and a man who wouldn't answer a simple question. "How did you hurt your leg, Dad?"

"What the hell does it matter?" He started pulling monitors off his chest.

How many times had they tiptoed around her mom's death? And did it really matter now? The details were obviously painful to him. And wouldn't she rather not know? *Look too closely and you'll see too much.*

"How did she die?"

Finger on the call button, he stopped. His eyes narrowed like they did when he bluffed poor old Walt. But he wasn't playing for pennies now. "What do you want, Lily?"

"The truth."

His façade cracked. Behind it she saw desperation—a gambler with one last bluff. "You were a little girl, I did what was best…. We've been over this a thousand times, Lily. She was killed by a drunk driver."

His limp, throwing out her mom's belongings. Not saying her name, refusing to drink. He couldn't even admit it to her now.

"That driver was you."

"Don't you dare judge me!" Anger flared and died. "There's more to it…."

"Tell me something to make me believe you again."

"She was leaving us."

"Us?"

She saw her mother clearly now, in a blue coat and white gloves and gripping that suitcase. Her eyes were cold. Angry. Lily reached out to her and cried, but her mom wouldn't look at her.

"She was abandoning you too, Lily."

"I don't believe you!"

He reached to touch the scar on her forehead. She drew back.

"I lost control of the car, but I saved you." He was begging now. "I'm not the one who abandoned you. Give me credit for that."

She owed him everything: her legal career—*Give that case to Sparks, she'll chase it down a hole!*—her meticulousness as a conservator, her entire view of the world. His protectiveness and concern, his pride in her successes and how she'd used what he taught. All a sham. He'd hated her mom. Worst of all, he'd taken away her chance to know her, to make her love her. To prove she deserved to be loved.

"We're two of a kind, Lily. She knew that and so do you."

Her perfect eye had blinded her. Not anymore.

Lily put the potatoes and corn back in the Boston Market bag and placed it in the trash. At the door, she turned. Whatever Harry Sparks was, he was no longer her father. She had one last thing to say to the stranger in the hospital bed.

"You didn't save me. The person I needed to be protected from was you."

———

Lily got in her Prius and drove. The night air was a balm. She found herself in the old neighborhood and parked across from her grade school. The anticipation of fall, the excitement of returning to class, the glee of recounting over supper what she'd learned that day. Her dad was a hero; everyone knew he'd saved that kid Gaylord by calling the cops after he spotted the abandoned ball. *Was any of it real?*

She drove to their street. This used to be a place where neighbors comfortably gossiped and watched over each other's kids. When a classmate later robbed a convenience store, they clucked, *What's this neighborhood coming to?* And when the housewife three doors down gassed herself in her garage, they talked about it for years. But nobody ever mentioned her mom. It was as if she never existed.

She left her car and walked the streets where they'd played his game. Chalk on the sidewalk, paw prints in the grass, the tab from a soda can. He didn't teach her to look to protect her. *He did it so I wouldn't see.*

One brick wall of the bungalow stood. The rest was a smoldering rubble. Were any of her mom's dishes left, or were they, too an illusion? She remembered searching the house for her belongings for years after she died, but he'd been ruthlessly thorough. The one thing he'd overlooked was the little gold compact with the galaxy and stars, and that was gone too. Next door, the McMansion glowed in the moonlight. A fine veil of ash had settled on it.

She drove downtown, past the cash-register shaped skyscraper where she'd practiced law, and to the museum. Framed against the stars, it looked more than ever like an extraterrestrial vessel blown wildly off course. *I'm the one who's lost.*

The one thing she wouldn't let go of was what she and Paul had shared. Driving past the Ritz-Carlton, she swallowed a Percocet dry to stave off the pain that made it hard to hold onto the wheel. When did she last eat? But the gnawing in her stomach wasn't hunger.

Where did she most want to go? *Back to the night mom died.* What if she'd run to her in that doorway, grabbed her knees and begged her to stay? What if she had another chance? To be a different person, to save her dad from himself? *To be the kind of daughter she would've wanted to be there for.* That fantasy was cruelest of all. Elena warned her not to look. Now she saw.

At the condo, she took two more Percocet. Just before they hit, she saw her attacker in her head. Felt, rather, him clambering over the rope at the Samurai exhibition and slowly circling the table in her lab. Something familiar...

"Jack?" she called. But he was with Louise. Her own bed was empty and far away. She grabbed an afghan and collapsed on the couch.

Chapter Forty-Two

Paul dipped his silver-handled brush in his shaving cream. He lathered his face and neck. In the bathroom mirror at the Ritz, he looked almost as lousy as he felt. After his two-day bender with Johnson, he could barely get out of bed; if not for his flight to D.C. he'd still be sleeping it off. Not that he had a choice. The FBI Director himself had ordered him to return, and it wasn't for a commendation.

How many bars did they hit after the Nick Lang fiasco? The last thing he remembered about Friday night was his fourth Jim Beam chased by beer and peanuts at some cop dive. They'd spent Saturday reviewing the case file for the last time before sampling the boilermakers at another set of bars. Johnson was divorced—three times—and Paul had a vague sense of having confided in him more than he'd intended. His bloodshot eyes said the rest.

You're too old for this.

As he dragged his double-bladed razor up his neck, his whiskers grated like static. He plowed on, his blade sawing like a scythe through a field of weeds. The first slip came at a sideburn. The second in the tender spot at the base of his nose. He repeated the process in the opposite direction. By the time he was done, his face was covered with toilet paper confetti.

Some hero you are.

Maybe Kurtz's murder was a one-off nut job. All he'd accomplished was to prove how ethically low he could sink and to destroy any chance he might've had with Lily. And now he was being recalled like an old Ford Pinto. Sure, he'd neutralized Nick. That thumb drive neutered him; with him holding it over his head, Nick wouldn't have the guts to contact her. At Johnson's urging, he'd tried to call her last night, regaining his senses sufficiently to avoid leaving a drunken maudlin message. Nick was right. He was ten years too late. He started to rinse his razor and brush, gifts from a woman at the Department of Justice he barely remembered.

Fuck 'em and forget 'em.

Self-loathing roiled his stomach. He threw the razor and brush in the trash.

He was to blame for her leaving law. And for upending the new life she'd made for herself by dragging her into the Kurtz investigation. Had he also cost her her job? There was a knock at his suite's outer door.

"Room service..." called a cheery voice. He hadn't ordered anything.

The door opened. Dishes clanked. The door closed. The Ritz was either concerned about the *Do Not Disturb* sign on his door for the past three days, or it was politely reminding him of checkout time. Ignoring the food, he donned an old grey T-shirt, Levi's and sneakers. He quickly packed. His eyes were gritty and when he rubbed his face shreds of toilet paper came off. Returning to the bathroom, he took a good look at himself in the mirror.

Is this who you want to be?

His laugh caught in his throat. Turning away, he saw something round and shiny on the counter, almost hidden amidst the Ritz toiletries. Her compact with the galaxy and stars. He ran his fingers over the lid. When he opened it, her woodsy scent rose like a whisper. He slipped it in his back pocket. He looked at his cell. More messages from D.C. and a dirty text from Johnson. He listened again to the two-second messages she'd left Thursday night. *Call me...* Nothing more from her. He stared at her number on his phone.

Didn't you hurt her enough?

That perfect eye of hers, the crazy game she and her father played. Funny thing was, it worked. She'd caught that line break in the Schiele all those experts missed. He wondered if she was right about Kurtz's killer. Was he a forger, had the murder been inspired by a painting? A Caillebotte landscape, for Christ's sake!

Can't let go, can you?

Closing his eyes, he played a game of his own. He went back and forth between the painting and the crime scene. Technique, palette, composition—something else linked them. Something that didn't belong.

What's hiding in plain sight?

But it was no good. He wasn't her. He put his service weapon in his carry-on bag and found his rental car keys. He did one last check of the room. In the trash was her ball cap.

The hat.

The one at the crime scene was a grey felt fedora with a broad brim and shallow indented crown. It was Kurtz's, but it didn't belong on the divan in the library. The man in *Seven* wore a farmer's hat with a wider brim and a taller crown. A long time ago, his own father had one like it, too. So what?

The killer likes old hats.

Paul chuckled grimly. But the fedora must mean something, or why leave it in the library? She was right: the crime scene was artistically composed. Every element had meaning to the killer. Was the hat his calling card? But if it belonged to Kurtz and not the killer—

He kept the real one.

If he could find the hat—and that damn beer can— he'd have the killer! He laughed again. Two needles in a Caillebotte haystack. Johnson was right. The hotshot from Quantico had blown it beginning to end.

He checked out and tipped the valet who brought his rental car. As he drove on I-70 to the airport, he kept thinking about Lily. Something else didn't make sense. She was damned good at her job, and despite being distracted by Nick, far too competent to allow a Degas to be destroyed. In the distance, the main terminal rose like sheets in the wind. In an hour he'd be up in that sky, and if he was lucky, tomorrow he'd be at his desk chasing a tax fraud or Ponzi scheme. But he couldn't stop thinking about her and the Degas.

Was she right, was she set up? No matter how insecure Gina was, he couldn't imagine her destroying a masterpiece to get Lily fired. If it wasn't an accident or Gina, was it connected to Kurtz? Kurtz had business enemies galore, but he'd always thought the murder had something to do with the museum. The violence and precision, the grotesqueness of the crime itself, said it was personal. He'd dismissed her every step of the way, but maybe she was right. If the killer was an artist who forged the Caillebotte, he'd want to see his painting every day. And she was a dog with a bone: if she went after him, getting fired wouldn't stop her. *Does she know how much danger she could be in?* He pulled to the shoulder. Cars whizzing past, he dialed a number on his cell.

"Gina?"

"Didn't expect to hear from you again, Paul." Kittenish, toying. He felt a pang of remorse. She deserved better than to be a distraction. "Dinner tonight?"

"I'm on my way to the airport."

"Oh. Next time, then."

Tell her what she wants to hear. He pulled out the compact and ran his finger over the swirls. So like Lily, that galaxy and stars. "I don't think so, Gina."

"You used me!" She waited for that old line to land. "It's Lily, isn't it?"

Tell her the truth.

"Yes." In the shocked silence that followed, he fiddled with the compact's clasp. It was loose; how many times had it been opened? "What happened with that Degas?"

"If you're begging for her job again..."

"Of course not, Gina."

She snorted. "Nobody entrusts a masterpiece to an assistant!"

"Assistant?" *Give me a name.* "But surely—"

"Amy's twenty-six years old!"

The copper-haired girl in the lab. He had the museum's directory on his iPad. If she still worked there, he could track her down.

"And this—Amy. What happened to her?"

"She came crying to me, of course. I had an opening for an assistant." Now all he had to do was scroll through the curator's staff. "You two belong together. You know what Lily tried to do to keep her job? Convince me *Seven*'s a fake.

She said she had proof!"
I better find him fast.

Chapter Forty-Three

It was Sunday afternoon when Lily rose. Her swaddled arm reeked and her hand was a baseball mitt. A dining room chair was shoved against her front door. *Did I do that?* Except for the hospital, the last thirty-six hours were a blur. She remembered being attacked and somehow thinking she could handle it herself. She rummaged in her refrigerator. A jar of pickles, some old cheese, a slimy artichoke. She drank a bottle of water and took two Percocet. Her attacker flickered in and out of her head. A shambling gait. Would he come back to finish the job? Not now, and not here. He'd wait until dark.

She vacuumed her carpet with one hand and tried to scrub the kitchen floor. She resisted going next door to visit Jack. She didn't want to bring grief to him or Louise. Should she let Kurtz's killer come to her? That was the Percocet talking. But she was just an afterthought; *Seven* was why Kurtz was murdered. What was the killer's grievance, what was his point? One thing was sure: His appetite for risk made him a gambler.

A fraud with a poker chip on his shoulder. Sound like anyone I know?

She almost laughed. In the meantime, no matter how angry and disgusted she was with her dad, he was her responsibility. Elena had told her to sleep on it. He could damn well cool his heels at Swedish until she figured out what to do next.

———

Poet's Row was a trendy area near the museum. The art deco buildings on Amy's block were named for literary figures. Hers was The Mark Twain. Paul knew getting what he wanted wouldn't be easy; his experience with twenty-something girls was less extensive than women scorned. And Amy had something to lose. He found her in the building directory and rang.

"Who is it?" Amy said through the intercom static. He answered unintelligibly. She buzzed him in. The copper-haired girl three flights up recognized him immediately.

"Oh!" Her hands flew to her cheeks. "You're Lily's FBI agent."

He smiled disarmingly and planted a sneakered foot on the doorsill. Behind her big eyes the wheels turned. "Can I come in?"

"What do you want?"

"To talk." He gestured at his T-shirt and Levi's. "This isn't official."

Past her shoulder he saw an oil painting of an elderly woman. Expensively framed, it dominated the room. Amy automatically stepped back so he could see better. From the threshold, he scrutinized the portrait. Every wrinkle and mole had been rendered with the remorselessness of a high-resolution photograph. He was no fan of hyper-realistic art, but even by its standards this painting was downright scary.

"She doesn't look anything like you," he said.

"Not yet, but she did win a prize." Amy smiled ruefully and stepped aside so he could enter. Her windows faced north. On an easel in the corner, away from that precious light, sat a smaller portrait of a copper-haired girl. One side of the face showed the skill of the prize-winning canvas. The other was a web of cracks.

"Work in progress?" he said.

"Maybe." Amy had circles under her eyes.

"Crappy week?"

"You could say that."

"Your work's pretty unforgiving," he said gently. "Too much realism can be unfair."

"An FBI art critic!" Her laugh was forced.

"Know what I see?" he said. "A girl whose life's just beginning. And an artist with talent to burn."

"Maybe ten years ago—"

"I have news for you, Amy. You can't be a has-been at twenty-six."

She sank onto the sofa bed. "Lily trusted me."

He sat next to her. "She doesn't blame you."

"She warned me not to use the spray bath!" She was about to cry.

"Why did you?"

"I—" She was protecting someone.

"Who loaded the varnish in the machine?" he said softly. "Nick?"

"Nick the geek?" She was genuinely confused. "He had nothing to do with it."

Shit. He regrouped.

"Look, Amy, no one's in trouble. I just want to understand."

"He was trying to help."

"Who?"

"He said if we used the spray bath, we could surprise Lily on Monday."

"Who?" he repeated.

"He offered to load it. I told him to use matte."

"Damnit, Amy! Who?"

"Dave."

What the…?

"Dave Byers," she said. "A senior docent at the museum."

Another dead end. *Go back to D.C. and hand in your badge.*

"He's my friend," Amy said, "the only one who really understands. You won't tell on him, will you?" she begged. "Lily likes him, too."

He started to rise.

"Dave knows his way around a lab, he's a chemist." She was practically babbling now. "He's retired, but he worked at Coors—"

He stopped. "Coors?"

"He feels worse about the Degas than I do. Any artist would."

"Artist?"

"Lots of docents paint, but Dave's a master. His oils should hang in a museum. He knows how it feels—"

To be a loser who can't sell his work.

"— and he's great to have a beer with. He brews his own."

Paul struggled to make his next question casual.

"And where does Dave live?"

———

At Swedish, a bouquet at the nurses' station wilted. Wheeled carts with trays of half-eaten food stood in the corridor, and a heart-shaped mylar balloon wafted forlornly from a door. Empty-handed—*forget Boston Market!*—Lily walked briskly down the hall to her dad's room. She flung open the door.

The room was empty. His bed was stripped. Even the wastebasket had been dumped.

"Where's Harry Sparks?" she asked the duty nurse. "I'm his daughter."

"Mr. Sparks was discharged an hour ago."

"Discharged?"

"He left against medical advice," the nurse said defensively. "He signed the waivers."

"Fuck the waivers! Why didn't you call me?"

"He instructed us not to."

Lily took a deep breath. "Where did he go?"

"A friend picked him up."

"My father has no friends!"

But he did. One who was a gambler, with a shambling, bearish gait. She heard his armor clank, smelled oil and metal and sweat. The sheer weight of him, pushing her onto the heat vacuum table... The carrot-haired nurse who thought her dad was such a charmer came out from the back. She smiled at Lily.

"His name was Dave."

Lily tried to clear her head.

They didn't bond because they were widowers. If Dave was ever married at all.

Their bond wasn't gambling, or art. It was a grievance against the world and an instinct for fraud. Would he harm her dad?

Or use him as bait?

He wants me.

Chapter Forty-Four

Dave's Dodge Ram was parked in front of his house. Lily drove past it to the dead end and parked at the barricade. To the west a tall fence strung with wire prevented access to Four Mile Park, now closed. Directly ahead lay the greenbelt. July's monsoons had thickened the scrub. Now it was brittle and dry. Across the ravine lay the bike path and walking trail. Beyond them, cottonwoods marked the plunge to Cherry Creek.

Dave likes him.

In the middle distance, a cyclist in a helmet and red jersey sped past a clutch of joggers and two women with a Saint Bernard. Soon the paths would be deserted. At dusk, foxes and coyotes went on the hunt. Past the cottonwoods and the creek, headlights flickered. Families returning from soccer games in the park.

What if he won't let him go?

Lily locked the Prius and crossed to Dave's property. From this direction, his lot was bigger than she'd thought. A chicken wire fence ran from his driveway to the ravine. At the corner farthest from the road the sun's last rays glinted like a mirror off the shed's metal roof. For an instant it seemed on fire. Then the light softened to a velvety glow that made the surrounding foliage black. Was that a lamp in the window? Like those '90s kitschy oils of cabins in the woods. Pay a little extra, and a master highlighter would add a splash of paint to make the work truly yours.

Dave's house was dark. The one next door looked

abandoned. Its owner had obviously cared for it. Neat flower beds had gone to weeds and the little doghouse was forlorn. A sign said *For Sale—New Price*. No help there.

Lily elevated her swaddled arm and slung her backpack over her good shoulder. She picked her way around Dave's house and down the slope towards the shed. The only light came from the shed; he'd wired it from his deck. She peered in the window.

Dave hunched over a sketchbook. Her dad sat across from him in an armchair with his bad leg hooked under. He was wearing a pair of old overalls that were too big. He looked dopey, lost. A little boy who'd awoken in a strange bed.

Leave now and go to the police.

But the way he sat made the hair on her good arm rise. *Pont's* dog with its leg cut off, Kurtz's broken ankles... Was Dave cropping her dad's frame? Those same hands rent Kurtz in two. If he'd caught her in the Samurai exhibition, her guts would have been on the gallery wall. She set down her backpack and opened the door.

They looked up in surprise.

Dave recovered nicely. "We were hoping you'd come."

"Speak for yourself," her dad said.

What could she use as a weapon? Long-handled gardening tools in the corner. At the far wall an easel, hanging next to it a rusted contraption and a beat-up hat with a tall crown and wide brim. A table with jars of brushes, tubes of paint, mixing trays, and a dispenser with a picture of a diapered tot in a field of grass. Baby Wipes. A thousand uses, from wiping a baby's bottom to... "Didn't know you had grandkids, Dave."

"I use the wipes to clean my palette knife." The chemicals on the blade that killed Kurtz.

Focus on Dave.

The sleeves of his frayed dress shirt were rolled over his elbows. One forearm was tied with a rakish bandana. His powerful knees straddling the stool made him look like Hemingway spoiling for a bar fight.

"It was nice of you to pick my dad up from the hospital, Dave."

"Niceness had nothing to do with it."

"Friendship, then. But his doctors—"

"Harry told me about your quarrel. Even a dutiful child has limits."

She turned to her dad. Could he walk? "You made your point, Dad. Let's go."

On the easel was a waterlily pond in the style of Monet. The palette and brushwork were right, but it was flat and lifeless. Too fulfilled. Dave hunched over his sketchbook. With her back to him, she slipped a brush from the jar on the table into the bandage on her arm. He pursed his lips and vigorously rubbed out a line. The cream paper was scored through and abraded by erasure marks. What remained evoked her dad, but the lines didn't flow. Without a master to copy, Dave couldn't create.

"*Seven* is your best work," she said. The little man was hubris, but he gave the painting a life of its own.

"And Caillebotte's." Dave shrugged modestly. "I like to think I have a Degas in me."

My poor ballerina.

Getting her dad up the slope would be dicey. Alone, he'd get lost in the dark, but freeing him evened the odds. "You painted *Seven* to prove a point," she said.

Dave's drawing hand tightened in a fist. His forearm tensed. The bandana was stained with blood. She remembered her scalpel plunging through muscle to bone and a wild exhilaration coursed through her. Their eyes locked. Dave set down his sketchbook.

"Your eye against mine, with Harry at stake?" He smiled. "Okay. What was my point?"

"To fool the experts."

"Why kill Kurtz?"

"Because he didn't care."

Dave drummed his pencil on his knee. "Why did I break his ankles?"

"Kurtz was the dog in *Pont de l'Europe*. The man who crippled you."

Dave looked stunned. Keeping her eyes on him, Lily reached behind her. "Put your arm around my waist, Dad." Dave still hadn't moved. With her good arm, she hoisted her father from the chair. He sagged. She braced his weight and said, "Count of three..."

Dave stepped forward with the palette knife.

With a rush of cool air the door opened.

Chapter Forty-Five

"Hi, Lily." Paul smiled crookedly.

The first things she registered were his Levi's and ratty T-shirt. Then what was he doing here, did he know who Dave was? The third was...

You came back.

"I'm Paul," he told Dave as if they were at a cocktail party.

Dave smirked. "I know who you are."

"Then you know I've come for Lily and Harry." Without seeming to move, Paul crossed the threshold. He took another step forward, and Dave waved the knife.

"Stay right there."

Paul held out his hands palms up to show he was unarmed. Stepping between Lily and the blade, he nodded reassuringly. His back was broad and strong. His sweat smelled like cloves. That palette knife would cut through his T-shirt like butter. In the back pocket of his Levi's was a small round object. Through the worn denim was the trace of a molded swirl. Her mom's compact? Fear coursed through Lily. Not for her dad or herself.

You damn idiot.

"This is quite a studio," Paul said. "I bet you don't miss Coors."

Dave chuckled. "I go back on occasion."

"Keeping your hand in, right?"

Dave laughed, relaxing his guard another notch.

Lily heard Paul think. *Assess, prioritize...Get Dave.* He gestured to her, thumb pointing to the door. He held up three fingers, made a fist, then held them up again. Minutes or count?

"Caillebotte should be grateful," Dave said. "I finished his series."

"And Kurtz?" Paul sounded so calm. "Is he the man heading into the storm, Dave?"

Paul gestured again, this time with two fingers. He moved closer to Dave, shielding her so she and her dad could get to the door. Dave seemed mesmerized.

"Can't say you didn't warn him, Dave," he continued. "What good's being a genius if nobody knows?" Step by step, he steered Dave to the far wall, all the while nodding calmly to Dave and gestured reassuringly to her. Dave was letting himself be maneuvered, but he had the knife. Did Paul know what that could do? But his priority wasn't Dave. Finally she saw. Not just saw, but knew.

He's brave.

"What's this?" Paul pointed to the jawed contraption on the wall.

"A leghold trap."

A heavy chain and padlock were attached. The chain was scratched and the padlock dented. Something, someone had tried desperately to get free. Those jaws weren't rusted. They were caked with blood. Old, and lots of it.

"What's it for?" Paul was buying time, drawing Dave farther from her.

Eyes unfocused, Dave answered in a hoarse nursery rhyme. The sing-song words were what a child sang to put himself to sleep.

"I caught a *varmint* by the *leg*, and *waited* then for him to *beg*..."

Kurtz's legs, cut from the frame. Her dad with his bum leg hooked under the chair. Something older—*Go now.*

Paul pointed to the farmer's hat next to the trap. "That your old man's, too?" They were at the wall by the tools. One was a machete with a wicked-looking pick. Paul kept talking softly. "I grew up on a farm, Dave. Was your old man a farmer, was that beet topper his? I bet he threatened you with it..."

He kept his back to her, screening her from Dave. The

cool air on her cheek said the door was steps to her left. Paul raised one finger to her, then reached in his back pocket. Dave unsteadily waved the knife in warning.

"He's the man in *Seven*—right, Dave?" Paul held the compact to the light and flashed it in Dave's eyes. Dave blinked. "Now!" Paul shouted.

Clutching her dad, Lily took three giant steps to the door. At the last minute she turned. Dave was coming at Paul with the machete.

No.

"Go, goddamn it!" Paul's hands were red.

Her dad's eyes pleaded. She was his only chance.

She dragged him out the door.

Chapter Forty-Six

They staggered to the road. It was pitch dark, the moon behind clouds.

"My leg…"

"I know, Dad. Let's get to the car." *Stash him there, call 911, get back to Paul.*

His hospital slippers flopped and he was heavier than he looked. He tripped on a root and it took all her strength to catch him. Lily put her good arm around his shoulder and braced his bad leg with her knee. With their dead weight as ballast and their sound limbs propelling them, they scrambled a three-legged race through Dave's obstacle course.

She focused four steps ahead, her feet remembering the terrain. *Visualize the Prius. 2007 silver hatchback with dents, remote in back pocket.* Left turn at the house, ten paces to the curb, Prius around the bend. The clouds parted and the moon peeked out. The Prius glinted. She reached for the remote.

Shit.

It was at the shack, in her backpack with her cell. She pried at the driver's door, kicked futilely at the hatchback to spring it open. She circled the barricade for a rock. Trigger the alarm… In the house across the street a light flickered. How long to rouse a neighbor? The light went out.

In the greenbelt something moved. A muskrat, or trick of the moon. On the far side of the creek, traffic lights and cars. Down the ravine, up the gravel, across the bike path, through the creek, then God knew what to the main road. Help was two hundred yards but a thousand miles away. Dave couldn't afford to let them go. By the time a driver stopped it would be too late.

Four Mile Park's fence was too high to scale. Between it and the barricade lay a narrow dirt path to the trails. To its right were the cement culvert and storm drains. The drain pipes were two feet wide and ran under the greenbelt to the creek. Was her dad scrawny enough to fit? They had to move fast.

"I've got a plan, Dad." She led him past the barricade. He saw the pipes and stopped.

"I'm not going in."

"Remember that kid on Gaylord?" She gave it a moment. It didn't matter if he'd really saved that boy; he could be a true hero now. "Who will we be if we abandon Paul?"

He dropped his arms. "It was an accident, Lily."

Mom.

"I know, Dad."

"She loved you. I put you in the car to change her mind."

Lily held out her hand and he took it. Together they slid down the culvert to the storm drains. He was dehydrated, exhausted and weak. He squared his shoulders and with a grim determination turned to the pipes. They looked dry. But rats and raccoons—even foxes and coyotes—needed a dark hole. *Make it a game.*

She gestured grandly. "Right or left?"

"Left."

"Look inside. What do you see?"

"Mud? It smells like sewer gas."

Kurtz was gassed. This was no game. "Details, please."

"Sticks and twigs. A nest." He crawled backwards into the pipe. "Bones and fur."

They exchanged a brisk nod.

"Keep your head high, Dad."

Chapter Forty-Seven

Willow roots, gravel, small boulders. She sped across the dark terrain. The shed loomed. Her backpack lay at the threshold. Inside was a hellscape by Hieronymous Bosch. Dave's easel and table were on their side. A shelf was torn from the wall, tools were scattered. In the corner Paul crouched, a bloody hand raised. Red bloomed across his chest. Dave towered over him with the beet topper.

No, no.

The knife was by Paul's leg. The shovel was too far to reach, but the leg trap was between her and Dave. She grabbed it by the chain. She swung it at the back of Dave's head. Flecks of dried blood flew. He dropped to his knees and his hair welled with blood. Slowly he turned. Surprise turned to betrayal and rage.

"Bitch!"

Dave grabbed the chain and yanked. Her injured hand was no match for his strength. She went flying to the floor by Paul. She scrabbled for the knife but Dave kicked it away.

"Who's perfect now, Lily?" he said.

She lay against Paul's thigh. Blood had seeped into his Levi's, the denim sticky on her cheek. Shakily he ran his fingers through her hair. She buried her face in his chest. He murmured something and dropped his hand to her shoulder. He didn't smell like cloves. He smelled like an iron nail dug from freshly tilled earth.

No, no...no.

She looked up at Dave. "It's a shitty painting."

"What? My Monet—"

"*Seven.*"

"It's Caillebotte's best." The beet topper's blade was honed. Its tip gleamed wetly. "Have some respect."

"It's unoriginal."

He snorted. "I made Kurtz into a landscape. How unoriginal is that?"

"*Seven* is as dead as Kurtz because it was painted by a fraud."

Dave reared back, and her hand slid to the knife.

"Fraud?" he bellowed. "All art is artifice!"

She slipped the knife to Paul and closed his fingers around it. He squeezed back, but barely. "Cell's in my pack," she whispered.

Get the bastard good and mad.

"Caillebotte twisted with the stick end of his brush, Dave. What'd you do with yours, poke? And your impasto's as watery as soup. Where'd you get such lousy paint?"

Dave quivered with rage. "I made those pigments!"

She lunged at him. He dropped the beet topper in surprise and she kicked it aside.

Take me, not Paul.

"Never good enough, were you?" She eased backwards. "That varmint knew it. Who was he, your—"

"Cunt!"

Dave two steps behind, she ran out the door. Greenbelt or road? One an obstacle course, the other a false haven. She'd never get past the ravine, but the road would lead him to her dad. She had to end it now.

She made for the ravine.

———

Lily slid down the slope, tearing her jeans on a rock. Thistles and weeds slowed her descent. A stand of cottonweeds marked the bottom of the dry stream bed, a rustic expressway for predators and prey. *Clump, clump whoosh.* Dave's thrashing said he wasn't far behind. The cottonwoods were the only shelter. She crawled to them and crouched behind the largest one.

The bark was dry and sharp-scented. She inhaled deeply, catching her breath. Catkins had turned to seed. White fluff tickled her eyes and nose. Something brushed against her hip. It had a hunched back and its fur was coarser than a dog's.

Don't look it in the eye.

The coyote loped off into the scrub.

Dave was at the edge of the trees. "Paul's dead, and I have Harry."

"You're lying."

"Come out and he's yours. Fair trade."

Was her dad in the pipe, or did he crawl out? If the gas didn't get him, Dave would.

"Last chance, Lily."

Flickety-flick.

She peered around the cottonwood. The jolly burgher in shirtsleeves and suspenders held a Bic lighter. The brush was tinder.

Now or never.

In the flame's halo, Dave's eyes did a crazy jig.

Dad chose the left hole.

She reached into the gauze on her arm and pulled out the paintbrush. It was a good one, an Isabey—the kind she used in her lab. The tip held a point. The ferule was nice and sturdy. Nothing but the best for Dave. But this wasn't really for him.

"This is for the ballerina."

She drove the paintbrush deep into his left eye and twisted.

Chapter Forty-Eight

Lily stood across from Michel's desk.

"The Caillebotte is forged," she said.

"*Non.*" His smile stopped short of his eyes.

Gina nodded in vigorous agreement with Michel. With Kurtz dead, *Seven* was her insurance policy. But Lily had Angela. *You have friends in high places,* Michel said when he refused to accept her resignation. *Pity about the Degas.* Lily held her temper.

"The forger confessed, Michel." And was proud of it. Dave planned to write a primer on Impressionism, including recipes for authentic paints. He even said where he got the canvas.

"*Non, non.*"

What would he do with all those T-shirts, mousepads, and coffee mugs?

"At least have *Seven* tested," she begged. "There are noninvasive scientific—"

"*Non, non, non.*" Michel rose to his full five feet, six inches, signaling the meeting was over. "Scientific analysis deceives. The eye is king."

In the kingdom of the blind, the one-eyed man ruled.

———

Lily put a final touch of glaze on the linden wood frame, then stepped back to examine it. Even under the lab's unforgiving light, the fine red gilder's clay glowed warmly through the gold leaf. The sixteenth-century cassetta frame was box-like, with a delicate inner molding and a frieze carved with vines and scrolls. It had taken a month to restore, but not too perfectly. It fit the Titian that The Kurtz Foundation was donating to the museum.

The Titian was a portrait of an old man with a long beard, piercing eyes and sunken cheeks. In his elegant skullcap and robe, he gazed into the distance. For most of his existence he'd resided in a seventeenth-century French Baroque frame with raised acorns and oak leaves. The Baroque was in good shape, but ornamental and dark. The dilemma was two frames: one in vintage condition, the other restored.

"Which frame does him justice?" Lily asked her new assistant.

"The cassetta's the right period," Matt said. "You calmed the patina with the glaze..."

"But?"

"It's a pity to junk the Baroque."

For an instant she missed Amy, who was back in school for a Master's in art history. But Matt had a good eye. Once he stopped seeing art through an economic lens, he'd be fine. Occasionally he needed a reminder.

"Remember what Degas said?" Lily prompted.

"The frame is the painting's pimp," he recited.

"Which pimp does the old gent deserve?"

Matt sighed. "The cassetta brings him to life."

She smiled at him affectionately. "The Baroque will find another painting to hustle."

As usual on Friday afternoon, the staff was gone. The graft on her arm was almost healed, and she slipped off the sling Elena had made from a swatch of Rosie's mulberry silk. Since Dave's arrest, her colleagues had kept a respectful but safe distance. Next week, when she shed the sling for good, the last visual reminder of Dave and Kurtz would be gone. She checked her cell for messages. Two from Paul in D.C. Poor baby!

The beet topper had missed his aorta, but he nearly bled to death and spent nine hours on the operating table. The FBI made a show of medevacking him when he was stable enough to move. Now he itched to return to duty. On her visits, the nurses fawned over him. But when he flew to Denver next month, he'd have to come to terms with Jack. Each had tangled with Dave and won. Her satisfaction was in taking the eye of the man who attacked them and destroyed the ballerina. That one-eyed king would paint no more.

The nagging issue was her dad.

He'd moved to a high-rise independent living complex near the Country Club. He groused about the food, but the ratio of widows to widowers was favorable. Whenever she saw him, he had a new periwinkled goddess on his arm. His refrigerator was filled with casseroles and pies, but her relationship with him had changed. Since that awful night in Dave's shack, the distance between them had become a gulf.

She grabbed her backpack and took the stairs to the European & American gallery on her way to the elevator. The gallery was deserted. At *Seven*, she paused. Eden before the storm greeted her like an old friend. But the man in the brimmed hat would not make it home. And what about the painting itself?

Forged paintings were pariahs. They were banished to deep storage, the lowest circle of museum hell. Did she want that for *Seven*? If it was alive, did it matter who painted it? Elena said art was a matter of perception. But could a lie ever be beautiful?

You can't make a fraud authentic by reframing it.

Were all frauds really the same? Lily thought of her dad climbing into the drain pipe so she could save Paul. She hit the speed dial on her cell.

"Dad? What are you doing for dinner tonight?"

Acknowledgments

I am deeply indebted to Mark Chimsky and Janette Macdonald for editing *A Perfect Eye*. Great thanks also to Susan Brienza, Jan Prince, David Miller, Meg Miller, Mara Miller, Honey Goldberg, Julie Hutchinson, and the writers at BONI for their wisdom and support.

About the Author

Stephanie Kane is a lawyer and award-winning crime novelist. She lives in Denver with her husband and two black cats. For more information, please visit www.writerkane.com.